PRAISE FOR THE EXTRA

THE FIRST BOOK IN THE OUTSIDERS SEQUENCE

"A nearly perfect, claustrophobic novella with a very effective countdown clock. If you have time for only one terrifying tale this spooky season, make room for *The Extra*."

—***The Wall Street Journal***

"*The Extra* is a fantastic calling card for the author. This is a mood book. And the mood is unbearable, slow-boiling tension. One of the most nail-biting endings of the year."

—***Grimdark Magazine***

"An absolutely killer premise executed with such slithery, sinewy care. After finishing Annie Neugebauer's *The Extra*, you'll find yourself carrying an additional fear you definitely didn't have before you started."

—**Nat Cassidy**, *USA Today* bestselling author of *When the Wolf Comes Home* and *I Know A Place*

"Neugebauer's *The Extra* is an exquisite and anxiety-inducing work of horror that had me vicariously stressed the heck out along with the protagonist. Worth every white hair it gave me."

—**Cassandra Khaw**, author of *Nothing but Blackened Teeth*

"Annie Neugebauer spins a disturbing tale of paranoia, identity, and horror packed with twists you absolutely won't see coming! Highly recommended!"

—**Jonathan Maberry**, author of *Burn to Shine* and *Cold War*

"*The Extra* is exceptional in every way: Extra unnerving, extra eerie, extra tense. Annie Neugebauer pedals in the same alpine paranoia as John Carpenter's classic *The Thing*, manifesting a sense of dissociative anxiety that only mounts with every turn of the page."

—**Clay McLeod Chapman**, author of *Wake Up and Open Your Eyes* and *Acquired Taste*

THE OTHER

THE OUTSIDERS SEQUENCE, #2

ANNIE NEUGEBAUER

THE OTHER

THE OUTSIDERS SEQUENCE, #2

SHORTWAVE

A SHORTWAVE BOOK

SHORTWAVE PUBLISHING
Publisher's full catalog available at:
shortwavepublishing.com

SIMON & SCHUSTER
Worldwide sales and distribution:
simonandschuster.biz

FIRST SHORTWAVE EDITION — JUNE 2026

COVER ART AND INTERIOR DESIGN
BY ALAN LASTUFKA

10 9 8 7 6 5 4 3 2 1

ISBN 979-8-89732-024-0 (Paperback)
ISBN 979-8-89732-025-7 (eBook)

An other one for Kyle.

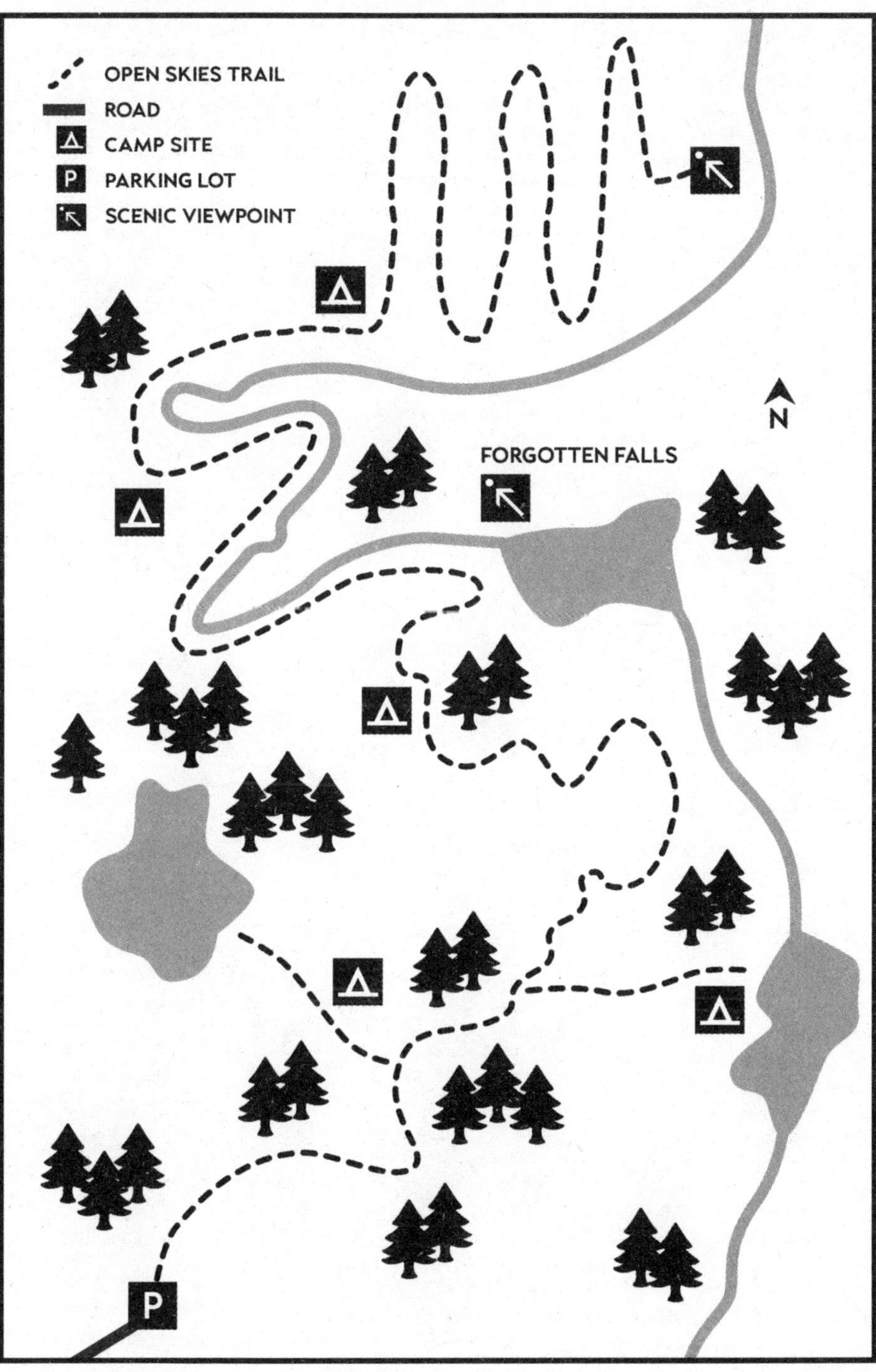
OPEN SKIES TRAIL
ROAD
CAMP SITE
PARKING LOT
SCENIC VIEWPOINT
N
FORGOTTEN FALLS
P

THE OTHER

THE OUTSIDERS SEQUENCE, #2

CHAPTER 1
ELISE

It's early enough in the spring that it's just the two of us out here. Turner Falls is probably already getting some traffic, since it's accessible by foot from parking lots, but Logan and I have found a smaller waterfall pool of our own. Not off-map or anything, but it's tucked a solid three-day hike back from any convenient parking, and we haven't seen a single other person out here our whole trip. The tiny parking pad was empty, and since this trail is a four-day-out and four-day-back hike and we're pretty fast, it's not likely that we'll bump into anyone.

I've never actually skinny dipped before, but there'll never be a better chance.

Logan's sitting on a fallen log tucking his socks into his empty hiking boots, wiggling his toes in the sunshine. Three days of hiking makes taking off our socks a thing of bliss. The air is cool, the sun warm, the rocky terrain makes a private little bowl for us, and the waterfall is both dramatic and unintimidating. It really couldn't be more perfect.

My husband stands, stepping out of his cargo pants and shucking his light layers. After a hesitation, he takes off his hat too. He has no tan yet. He grins at me over his shoulder before easing into the little blue-green pool. The joking yelp he gives lets me know the water is still winter cold, and we won't be swimming for long.

The little pool is ringed in large, craggy boulders that jut from the decaying leaves. Between them, little patches of green shoots spring up.

I strip down and wade in. The cold on my feet is like a fresh breath, but it only takes a few more steps before I'm questioning the decision. The heat from our hike has given me a false sense of temperature. This is seriously cold.

There's a second where I consider backing out and saving my delicate bits from the plunge, but I'm not going to leave Logan alone in the buff. With a bracing gasp, I dive in.

He's laughing at me when I surface, so I splash him. He yells and splashes me back, I tackle him, he spins me: it's all very cute. Laughing, we sink into a deep hug. I press my shivering body against his, and he's big and warm and comfortable. My Logan.

Nearby, several different birds are making a pretty racket, taking turns singing their songs.

I allow us a few moments. I take a deep breath, let it out on a sigh.

It's nice to be cute together. That's one of the problems, that we don't spend enough time together anymore. One of the issues we came out here to work through. So maybe we cross one off the list?

Of course, we can't take a ten-day vacation every time we start to drift apart.

I'm underplaying it. This is more than drifting apart. This is make-or-break. This is decision time. This is the rest of our lives.

I pull out of our hug and start "taking a bath" while I'm in here. No soap, but a good rub down of the sweaty areas. Maybe we'll stink less when we zip up the tent tonight. Logan follows suit, sensing my shift in mood. Fifteen years together will do that. We can read each other's micro-cues without even trying.

Our skin is rigid with gooseflesh. He dunks his hair under, and I start wading back to the rocky shore. The mud at the bottom of the pond is so soft it feels like a cloud. I hurry onto the sand and then the rocks to dry off on my meager camp towel. Backpacking means packing as light as humanly possible, which means there's not even enough towel to spread out and lie down on. Instead, it's one of those weird quick-drying squares of mystery material. I dry off fast and climb back into my clothes before laying down with my backpack as a pillow, closing my eyes.

The birds nearby are loud, clear above the sound of the waterfall.

Whatever we decide, I'm glad we did this. We needed this time together, just us two. We owe each other this level of intentionality. I just turned thirty-two. He's thirty-three. We've been together since we were in high school, married young but just because we knew it was the right fit, not because we were rushing. We always thought we wanted kids and assumed we'd start when we hit thirty.

Thirty came, and we were trying to wait out the pandemic. Thirty-one came, and I was switching career fields. Thirty-two came, and the whole world seemed on fire around us, sometimes literally, and we just kept. . . not starting. It's been long enough that I have to ask myself if the reason we're not starting is because we don't really want to. What if we just *assumed* we wanted kids? What if we don't actually? Or worse, what if one of us doesn't and the other does?

My eyes are clenched tight. I force myself to ease, to just let them be closed and not squeezed. But I feel the muscles in my face fighting to frown.

What if it's me?

What if Logan is ready and I'm the one holding us up? What if I'm never ready and I just hold him back and hold him back until it's too late? I don't want to hold him back. I love him too much. And I think he loves me enough to let me. I really do. Which means if anyone is going to set him free, it will have to be me.

A tear slips from my loosely-clenched eye, and I sit up.

He's wading out of the pond, hurrying to his own camp towel and clothes. He's a tall guy, lanky with a little belly, very handsome. Pale skin, thick dark hair. He has one of those smiles that you automatically return, a dimple in only one side.

He settles down beside me when he's dressed. "Noisy little guy," he says, and I follow his gaze to a small gray and white bird perched on a dead branch that juts up from a tangle of bristly bush. Its beak is open on a series of whistles but then opens again to make a higher burst of trills, followed by a few croaking rasps.

"I totally thought that was a bunch of different birds," I say.

It hoots four times in rapid succession and moves on to another type of trill.

"He's good," Logan says, and I smile at the way it sounds like credit where credit's due. Then he looks at me where I hover between a sprawl to soak up sun and a huddle to hold myself. "Cold?" he asks.

I shake my head, even though I am a little, because I know he'll offer me his jacket, and he should wear it. He often thinks of me first.

He's born to be a dad. It's innate. I think he'd say the same about me, and maybe I would too, if we were in a different time. A time of tribes and support systems. Or at least a time of staying home, one-income families, an economy that sustained such things. But I've watched friend after friend slip away into motherhood. They're over-busy, and their health is never the same. No matter how thoughtful their husbands are, they end up isolated. They don't seek a tribe. They don't find support. They don't thrive.

I don't want to lose me to make someone new.

I open my mouth to ask Logan something—to say anything, really, to breach this topic. We came out here to talk through this, to really hash it all out and feel the hard things and say the deep things and make a decision—but he speaks first. "Those rocks up there kind of remind me of that one building in Madrid that looked like it was melting."

I glance at him, then to the rocks he points at above us. They do look like they're melting down the top edge of the waterfall, smoothed and glossed by water over a long time. "You mean in Porto?"

He shakes his head. "It was a cathedral, I think. In Madrid."

I give him a sideways look. "I think I know the one you mean. On that college trip. It was in Portugal, though. Our tour group didn't go to Madrid."

Now it's his turn to look confused at me. "I would've sworn it was Madrid." The way he says it tells me he still would; he thinks I'm wrong.

But he's mixed up. It crosses my mind to point out to him that the only capital city we went to in Europe was Paris, so it couldn't have been Madrid, but what's the point? It's been over ten years since we went on that group tourism thing, and we only stayed in each city for like a day. Easy to blur all the statues and buildings and landmarks together. "I remember the cathedral you're talking about, where the stone looked like wax. The rocks do look like it."

He gives me a soft smile, and I can practically read his thoughts that he wants to dig up those old photos when we get home. If we split up, who would all those go to? The concept of trying to divvy up our life together, our history and belongings, it strikes me as a practical possibility for the first time. We've been together so long, grown up around each other. It makes me feel grief-wild just imagining it.

He stands, offers me his hand to pull me up. "We still have a mile left to get to a decent spot to make camp. Let's hit it before dusk sneaks up on us." The little bird continues its barrage of songs, each one short, loud, and eerily distinct, like a bird radio being tuned.

Nodding, I follow Logan away from this little paused paradise and back toward the trail.

CHAPTER 2
LOGAN

Elise's black hair has dried into my favorite, which I only ever really get to see when we're camping or caught in a rainstorm or something unexpected: an entire halo-layer of soft fuzzy curls that spring from her double French braids. I know she hates it, but I think it's literally one of the prettiest things about her. One time I called it cute, and she almost shanked me.

I walk behind her, because I'm too tall to set our pace. Plus, she likes to slow down a lot to look at views or animals or logs covered in moss. She always stops to point them out to me. I love seeing things through her appreciation. She'll make a great mom, if it comes to that.

I'm not so sure it will anymore. I saw the resignation on her face at the skinny dipping pool. I have this knot in my guts that tells me by the end of this trip she's going to ask for a divorce.

I keep taking in these woods, trying to soak it up and appreciate them, because someday I might look back on this and savor it as the trip that saved our marriage. If it goes the other way, though, I may never want to go backpacking again.

I'm amazed by how different this part of Oklahoma is from the other parts I've been to. Usually, Oklahoma just looks like a continuation of Texas to me, but this one little swath of "mountain" is genuinely a different terrain. Like Texas and Colorado blended. The height of the peaks themselves is no big thing, but the elevation changes are so much more extreme than anything in Texas. Rises jut abruptly up and drop sharply down in a way they don't back home.

The trees are different too. Not entirely—there are still oaks galore and plenty of undergrowth to snag at clothes—but there are also pines here, soaring taller than I'm used to. It makes it feel like we've really traveled somewhere new, even though we only drove an hour and a half north to get here.

We head up what I hope is the last incline for the day, because my shins are killing me. And my shoulders. And my back. It's almost like I'm not so young anymore.

I think that might be part of what Elise is worried about. The whole physical decline part of becoming pregnant and a parent. The intimidation of labor, the exhaustion of nursing. That makes sense. I wouldn't be keen to sign up if I was the one who had to do the bulk of it either, and I'm certainly not going to pressure her. Everyone is so judgmental of mothers too. Work and you're abandoning your kids; stay home and you're lazy. It's a damned if you do situation in a way it's just not for dads. If she wants to travel as we get older instead, I'm game. I can be content with anything as long as it's with her.

Except for her being unhappy. I can't stomach that.

Ahead of me, Elise pauses to pull out her blaze-orange beanie, and I realize it has started to get chilly already. It's not six yet, but later than we meant to make camp tonight. I dig out my hat too, an old forest green one that cuffs at the bottom. Hers is that new style that always looks comical to me, like an elf with the extra material at the top.

"Excuse me, small ma'am? Do you know which tree they make the cookies in?"

She gives me a side smirk as she hauls her big backpack on again with a groan. Her camp towel swings from it, drying on a carabiner. "It's the style, gramps. Maybe if you sprang for a hat manufactured this decade, you'd have warmer ears."

I can't find the quip fast enough. Something about pointy ears? "Overconsumption is a downfall of modern society!" I say, and she snorts as she starts back up the trail.

I'm looking at where I place my boots, still trying to find the joke about hats and elf ears when I bump into her backpack. She's stopped in front of me without warning. I reach out instinctively to steady us both, and she says softly, "Whoa."

The ground ahead of us is grass. On the trail itself, which is packed dirt and dead leaves every time of year, the ground is bright, vivid green grass. Plush as a lawn.

From down trail, below it, I can see the overall shape. It's very neatly overlapping circles. Two perfect circles about six feet across each but merged in the middle. A vertical Venn diagram.

There's no way it's incidental, right? No one plants grass out here, and wild grass isn't this neat, isn't this green, and it's certainly not on the trail in a clear shape. There's no grass outside the combined circles, no stray sprigs growing outward.

It is early spring, so some of the plants coming back to life are that almost neon shade of green that seems unreal, but to see such a strong patch of it all together is another level. There are small buds on the trees and shrubs, little dots of color, but this?

Shocking.

"Wow," I say. Not entirely sure why, I suggest, "Go around?" It's just so surprising that I don't want to walk on it.

Elise nods, edging off the trail into some weeds and undergrowth to go around it. Once we're back on the trail, looking down, I see that the grass has holes in it. That's the only way I can think of it. If the spread of it was a florescent green blanket, it's a crocheted one, with gaps and lines in patterns I can't quite follow. They look geometric, though. Like a big stamp of some foreign text. I wonder, if I were up in the sky looking down, if I could read it, but I doubt it. It strikes me as indecipherably other.

"Bizarre," I mutter, and we trudge tiredly up the trail.

After a few minutes, Elise pauses and says quietly, "There's someone up ahead."

My eyebrows lift as I crane my neck to see what she's seen.

There's the bright color-blocked motion of others moving along the trail ahead, headed slightly downhill between the trees at some distance. I can hear them now that we're still, listening for it, but I hadn't before. I think I see two hikers, moving towards us. Odd, because no one was parked at the trailhead when we got here, and it's an out-and-back. I can't see how anyone could've passed us. Even if they were hauling ass coming up behind us, we would've heard them. Maybe they cut through a section of woods with no trail?

We both hold still for a few moments, watching them approach, but then I realize that's a bit weird. When you cross someone on a trail there's no way to avoid at least a polite nod as you pass each other. If we're lucky, they'll just wave and hustle on their way. If we're not, they might want to make small talk about what awaits us up ahead or even try to barter for something. It happens. People run out of toilet paper or whatever and try to trade.

Elise must arrive at a similar inevitability, because she resumes trudging up this section of trail. It spills us into a flat area that I realize must be the campsite we've been headed for. My attention split between the approaching hikers—two, it looks like, or maybe three if that's a baby they're carrying—and the site, I pick out a campfire ring and a couple of bare areas that would hold a tent.

"Howdy," a voice calls out from the trees, followed by a feminine, "Hi!"

"Hey," I answer back.

Elise follows with a friendly, "Hello."

Now that we have the four cornerstones of Oklahoma greetings accounted for, there's not much more to do than sort of shuffle to the side to let the other couple cross through. It occurs to me, though, that they might not want to cross through. It's near dinner time, and they were probably headed down to this same campsite for the evening, which means we'll either have to share or press on way later than will be nice. Hiking in the dark is not fun, and the next designated campsite is a couple miles farther up or even farther back. "Shit," I mutter under my breath. There isn't enough time to ask Elise what she prefers without risking them hearing us whisper and thinking we're rude.

Elise is a pretty private person, especially while camping, so I'm a little surprised when I hear her give out a friendly chuckle. "Nice hat!" she calls to the young woman leading the other couple into the open area.

She's wearing the exact same bright orange beanie Elise is. She looks at us, staring at Elise, and raises a hand to feel her own hat as if her hand will remind her what it looks like. She cracks a grin. "You too!"

The guy that towers behind her looks across at me, points to his own head. "Hey, you too man. A classic."

I also raise my hand instinctively, but of course I recognize my forest green rolled hat on his head. It's a super common color for beanies, but his might even be the same vintage version as mine. I smile. "If it ain't broke, don't fix it, right?"

We all sort of chuckle, as if they, too, have had the similar playful banter about their hats, and it's nice to have an icebreaker as we all pool together at the campsite. They're young, probably about thirty as well. The woman is shorter than the man, like us, and her dark brown hair trails out from her hat in a single side braid. The man is about as tall as me, but bigger, strong looking. What I'd thought might be a baby in one of those chest rigs is just his backpack that he'd swung around front to get something out of. We all have on the sort of standard spring outdoor apparel: cargo pants, hiking boots, layers of tops and zip-up fleece, plus our backpacks.

"Whoa, nice quarter-zip too," the woman says, indicating Elise's sweater with a nod, and I realize that's also almost the same. The other woman's is light purple, and Elise's is sky blue. They both have on gray pants and brown boots.

I look at the guy and see that he and I are also almost matching. We both have fleece jackets with the neck open around plaid shirt collars. I study his face for a second and find him to also be a palish white guy. I can't tell what color his hair is under his hat, nor he mine, I guess.

There's an awkward sort of silence as we all check each other out, scanning for similarities.

Finally, Elise says, "Well I've always wanted to meet my doppelganger."

The other woman, eyes wide, says, "Me too. Or are you ours?"

Elise shrugs, and they both make that weird sort of noise sound that alludes to, but is not quite, a laugh.

"Well," the other guy drawls. "I must say, you both have impeccable taste."

That makes me laugh, and I see Elise visibly relax at it, and then we're all laughing. They seem nice, easy humored. I shake my head, holding out my hand for a shake. "Logan," I introduce myself.

He takes the handshake, hand fitting seamlessly into mine. "Bryce. This is Allison."

Allison waves, dodging the shake-patrol, and Elise introduces herself.

"So, I reckon y'all were headed to this campsite for tonight?" I ask, trying to make it sound open and friendly rather than inconvenienced. I'm still doing mental calculations trying to decide what Elise would rather do: press on or share with strangers.

"We were," Allison says, "but if you two wanted this one to yourself we'd be happy to keep going. Wouldn't hurt to get a bit farther down the trail. Do you happen to remember how far the next spot is?"

"It's a good seven or eight miles down trail," I admit. "And back y'all's way?"

Bryce says, "Maybe three."

I glance at Elise. She shrugs. "We could keep going, if y'all were trying to do your own thing?"

It's not a clear rejection, so the awkwardness softens a bit more. "We don't mind," Allison says, smiling. "We've already had several nights to ourselves. If you guys want to share a campfire, we'd be game."

That means no Big Talks tonight, and we've already been stalling and postponing it every night. I mean, we've talked around the issues some, but we haven't really dived in and tackled them head-on the way we set out to do when we planned this trip. We could force it, hike for another hour into dusk and then hustle to set up at the next campsite, but will we really feel like getting into it then either? After an exhausting last leg and pitching tents in the dark?

"Why not?" Elise asks, glancing at me. "Okay with you?"

Of course, I'm not going to say no now. And a part of me is relieved at the reprieve of another night before what I'm increasingly fearing will be the Big Fight. No, not looking forward to that at all. One more night sounds good to me.

"Yeah, let's do it," I say.

CHAPTER 3
ELISE

The other couple don't seem like serial killers, so I think we'll be okay. They take the up-trail tent spot, and we take the down-trail one, so that the campfire spaces them out nicely, and no one makes it weird. It's wild how much they look like us, but it gives us something to talk and joke about.

After we both pitch our tents, the man, Bryce, asks Logan if he wants to help him gather firewood, and although that's vaguely more menfolk-y than we would've played it, they head off to gather logs and branches while Allison and I compare notes on what food we've packed.

"So, how are y'all coming this direction?" I ask while I rummage for the food in my backpack.

Allison looks at me from where she's digging through her own backpack. Her eyebrows dip down from the bottom of her hat, furrowed. It's hard to tell from here, but I think her eyes are dark brown like mine. "What do you mean?"

I hesitate, suddenly feeling like I've asked something intrusive, but I don't know why. There's nothing personal about it. Maybe it's because I'm thinking of how we came close to being caught skinny dipping after all. "Well, we haven't passed each other yet," I say, "and there were no cars parked at the trailhead."

She cocks her head at me, and the gesture makes me realize I've done the same to her first. She's mimicked me, probably trying to figure out what I'm asking. Odd that it's not clear.

She hasn't answered.

The wave of discomfort swelling is so unpleasant that I look down at my bag just so I don't have to look at the stranger in front of me. I wish I hadn't asked, but now that I have, I have to push through. "Did you have someone drop you off at the trailhead?" I prompt.

"Oh!" She has a big smile on her face. I smile back reflexively. "We had someone drop us off!"

My smile hangs there, waiting for her to say more, to flesh out the explanation. Probably something about not wanting to leave a car with a finicky battery, or loaning it to a friend, or whatever. Maybe a note about who dropped them—friend, roommate, parent. But she doesn't explain. She doesn't say anything.

"Oh," I say, my smile congealing along the edges. My hand finds the rigid edge of the freeze-dried backpacking meals we brought, so I seize on the excuse to change the subject. "Looks like we're having chicken parmesan tonight. What did y'all bring?"

She pulls out a bag of noodles and a pouch of beef jerky. "Breakfast of champions."

We both laugh, but mine feels canned. "I'm going to go

'unpack' in our tent," I say, immediately feeling dumb for having explained it. It's odd though. To just walk away might've seemed abrupt, but to tell her what I'm doing makes it seem like we're here together on a group trip.

"Good idea," she says, and I expect her to head to their tent too, but she just keeps rummaging through her pack. Did she mean good idea that I go?

I'm beginning to wish I'd taken Logan's subtle offer for us to keep hiking to a private site. The last thing I want to do at the end of a long day is sit around and stew in strange social dynamics.

Stifling a groan at the weight, I grab my backpack and lug it over to our tent. I unzip, dump it in, and after a second thought, I grab Logan's too. Maybe it seems like I'm worried they're going to steal from us if I'm not watching. Hopefully it just seems like I'm unpacking his things too. I'm not entirely sure which is the main reason. It might be neither—just that I wish now I had more privacy and the closest I can get is bringing in our stuff. As I zip myself into the tent, I glance at Allison one last time. She's rummaging through her own backpack, but in a way that reminds me of an actor on a stage or set. Like she's trying to look like she's searching for something but is actually just shifting things around until I'm not watching.

I swallow a dry lump in my throat and finish the zipper. What's wrong with me? They've been nothing but pleasant since we ran into them. She probably has minor social anxiety or something. Shaking my head at myself, I set about actually getting us settled in here, since that's what I said I was going to do. I unfurl and fluff up both sleeping bags, inflate the pads that go under them, arrange the small space with our clothes as pillows. I even drink the rest of my bottle of water and grab the filter for a refill at the creek.

I don't want to go alone though. And I don't want Allison to tag along.

Thankfully, I hear the guys come back and the clack of fire-wood being stacked. Logan asks, "Where's Elise?" and I force cheer into my voice to call out, "I'm in here!"

I grab his bottle from the pocket in his pack, the pot for our stove, and bring them all out, holding up the filter. "Come with me?" I ask Logan.

He glances at me, back at them, then toward the creek. "You bet." To the other couple he adds, "Be back in a minute."

Bryce waves, bent over the fire ring getting things set up.

Allison still squats at her backpack, facing away from us, a long braid trailing down her back. She hovers with her wrists draped over her knees, observing him. She doesn't turn to watch us walk away, but I still have the impression that she's listening to track our movement. Like if we stopped or detoured, she'd notice right away.

Totally normal to be hyperaware of strangers. Hell, look at me. I resist looking back at them as we move down toward the creek.

CHAPTER 4
LOGAN

I can tell something's wrong before Elise even says anything. She's waiting until we get some distance from Bryce and Allison, which means she doesn't want them to hear whatever she's going to say, which is enough to tell me something's on her mind.

The woods at dusk are always sort of hushed. Not quiet—there's plenty of movement around us when we hold still long enough to pick it out—but sort of breathless. Every animal of the day is hurrying to finish their tasks and head back to the safety of some shelter, aware that the animals of the night are stirring, stretching, beginning to prowl.

There's still plenty of light to see the creek streaming over rocks and logs, to begin to pump water through our little handheld filter, but it's the kind of light that sneaks away without warning. Above us, in the glimpse of deepening sky afforded by the creek, strangely flat clouds in deep purple hover off in the distance, like cardboard cutouts someone taped up.

Elise is still quiet, probably trying to figure out how to say whatever it is she's worried about. Honestly, it doesn't matter to me what it is if it matters to her.

"It's not too late for us to take off," I say quietly. "I can come up with a reason."

She looks at me, eyes big with relief. "It's almost dark."

I shrug. "We have headlamps. A night hike might be fun. Memorable."

She forces a small smile but shakes her head. "We'd have to repack the tent and everything."

I can't tell how far she wants me to push this. Sometimes Elise has a hard time being the one to decide. I can help her get there if I know what she wants to do and is just in her way, but I'm not sure if she actually does want to leave, or if she just wants to have voiced doubt. "Did she say something?" I ask.

"No, no," she concedes, capping her bottle and grabbing mine. "She's nice. A little odd, maybe. When I was asking about them getting dropped off at the trailhead, she was sort of withholding."

"What do you mean?" I ask. "Bryce told me they hiked through off-map to meet the end of the trail."

She stops pumping the filter. "Are you serious? She told me someone dropped them off at the beginning."

"No, he definitely told me they bushwacked through an undeveloped section to find the trail. They primitive camped and everything."

"I don't understand. Why would they lie?"

I frown, move to take the filter from her stalled hands, but she bats me away and hands me my bottle instead. Then she starts pumping water into our cooking pot, a small metal cannister. I muse, "Maybe Allison didn't want to tell you they went off-trail in case we're really strict on park rules? Like we'd get them in trouble with rangers or something?"

"I guess," she murmurs, but she's obviously not convinced.

A bird somewhere above us has a strange call, reminiscent of a mourning dove or owl, but it could be another mockingbird, sounding larger than it is. I look through the newly-green leaves but can't find it in the growing dim. It's so much darker from beneath the trees than when I look up to the sky itself.

After she finishes filling my bottle , Elise asks, "When he told you they cut through, did he come up with that answer, or did you prompt him?"

"I asked him."

"Right. But did you suggest the answer before he actually said it? Like when I asked her, she didn't have an answer right away, so I offered one, and she just sort of agreed with me."

I think back. We were breaking limbs off a fallen tree, and I asked him how they'd gotten ahead of us on the trail. "I guess I did suggest it? I think I did. I'm not sure. What's. . ." I hesitate, not wanting to sound dismissive. "What is it that you're worried about?"

"I don't know," she says in exasperation. I'm not entirely sure if it's aimed at me or her. "I just feel uncomfortable."

"We can go," I say again. "We don't have to stay here, babe. We don't owe these folks anything."

I can see the resignation settle on her shoulders. "If it was still light, I'd say okay. But in the dark? I don't think it's worth it. Let's just get through dinner and turn in early. I'm exhausted anyway."

I offer my hand to pull her up. When she stands, I tug her into a hug. "Me too," I say. "We'll get a good night's sleep, and we can hit the trail at first light."

Her cheek rubs my chest when she nods, but her arms cling to me just a little too tightly.

CHAPTER 5
ELISE

The sound of the creek fades into the background as we approach camp and is eventually overtaken by the crackle of a campfire. Because of the angle we approach from, I hear it before I see it. I don't hear any talking. I realize that we've neared quietly, as if to catch whatever conversation they're having, but there's none. Not wanting to startle them, I clear my throat and let my footfalls land heavier as we crest the little rise to get to the site.

They're both sitting down low, on logs or rocks or small camp stools, facing the fire across from the trail where we are. They both turn their faces to look at us, me in front of Logan, and for just a second, I have the utterly uncanny sensation of seeing ourselves sitting there instead of strangers. The man, Bryce, looks so much like Logan in the firelight that I hold my breath, searching his features until I can pick out a difference. His nose is broader, his jaw softer. But damn, it's really remarkable.

"Hey," I squeak, immediately clearing my throat.

They both smile, and Bryce has two dimples. Logan only has one.

"We're not actually using the fire for our meal," Allison says, tilting her head to a single-burner camp stove that has a pot balanced on it. "So, we made it nice and big, but if y'all want to cook on it we can shove it over for some coals."

"Nah, we're just boiling water," Logan says, coming around from behind me and heading to our tent, presumably to grab our collapsible camp stools. "Thanks, though."

I gather our supplies from where I left them earlier and pull my headlamp out of my pocket and hang it around my neck, turning it on to balance the pot and light the burner. Dark has settled quickly, building between trees to obscure the woods and enclose the campsite like a private room. I listen to the rush of the stove lighting, the small jet-propellor sound of it heating the water intensely fast. I open the two bags while I wait, scrunching my nose at the chemically smell of the meals. I'm super ready to have fresh food again, but hungry enough that I'll eat this whole thing for sure.

Logan emerges from our tent with the stools, and I watch him heading toward the fire, trying to decide where to set them up. He opts for across from the other couple, us near each other and the fire without crowding things. Pretty much what I would've chosen.

When the water is at a rolling boil, I turn off the stove, wait a second, and use the handle to carefully pour it into the two open bags. Logan comes over and grabs one, sticking a spork in it, and hands me the second utensil. We silently carry our super-hot dinners to the fire, stirring them at our feet.

Across from us, the other couple have already started. There are soft slurps as they eat their noodles from metal camp cups, and the smell of jerky reaches me even from across a fire. I eye my pouch hungrily, but I've burned my mouth more times than not by starting too soon. I pick it up and stir it more, trying to help it cool faster.

The crickets have begun their nightly screeching, louder than seems reasonable, all around us. The sound redoubles the sensation of being enclosed here, a living wall, like our campsite is a bubble of civilization.

"So," Bryce says, "how long have you two been together?"

"Almost sixteen years," Logan says proudly.

Allison says, "That's even longer than us!" Then she squints at us. "But how old are y'all?"

I laugh. We get that a lot. "We were high school sweethearts," I explain. "How about you guys?"

She looks at him, smiling. "We were college sweethearts, I guess. So going on ten years?" She lilts at the end of it just enough to make it a confirmable question.

Bryce just shrugs, nodding.

So, they're probably between twenty-eight and thirty-two.

Bryce asks, "Married?"

"Yeah," I say. "Y'all?"

"Mhm," Allison affirms. I glance at her hand, but see no ring. His either. That's still normal. Lots of people take them off for outdoor stuff like camping. We have the silicone ones that we switch to for trips like this. Allison asks, "Where'd you go to school?"

"UT," I answer. Then I point to Logan. "Texas Tech."

“Oh man, we’re from Texas too,” Bryce says. “I went to UNT, Allison to A&M.”

“Wow,” I say, voice flat. I can’t shake my weirdness. I have the unfounded feeling that they’re just copying our answers. I try to think of a question to ask so they have to answer first, but right as I’m mentally rummaging around in the ‘what do you do for work’ grab bag, a pair of eyes flashes in the woods behind the other couple.

I gasp, and everyone turns to look. Several different headlamps illuminate a small, furry body slinking away between trees. Low to the ground, maybe a possum or fox. It makes almost no sound as it disappears from sight, startled by our lights.

“A visitor,” Allison quips, keeping the tone light, but my heart is pounding.

I’m not afraid of small animals, or the dark, or the wilderness per se, but there is something about being out here at night. The illusion of being protected by “walls” of shadow between trees has been broken. This space that felt cozy and lit by our fire’s glow is not enclosed. It’s surrounded.

My mind zooms abruptly out and out and out, and the forest stretches for miles in every direction, and all of it is open to itself, and anything inside it can cross into this space.

We are not alone out here.

The urge to look over my shoulder is irresistible. I shoot my light into the woods behind me, but nothing visibly stirs there. Yet a hundred crickets screech in one overlapping, continuous scream that reminds me of a very distant alarm.

The eeriness of it has crept under my collar, and I fight not to pull up my hood, as if that one layer might ward off something sneaking up behind me. "Did you guys hear about that group that was out here last fall? It was a group of girls. Maybe a youth group? Or older. A bachelorette party?"

Bryce leans forward, eager for what must sound like the beginning of a campfire story. Which I guess it is, but this one is true. My coworker told me her sister was best friends with one of the girls.

Allison says, "No, what happened?"

Logan offers, "It was a sorority."

"That's it!" I snap my fingers. "A sorority group. They came out here to camp and brought home a stranger."

Bryce frowns. "A group of young women? That doesn't sound safe."

"Well, the stranger was a young woman too, their age. But that's not what's weird. What's weird is that they all swore they knew her, and that she was part of their club. But when they got back to campus, no one else there had ever heard of her. There was no record of her being a student, no ID, no friends, nothing."

"Whoa," Allison breathes. "So, she, like, tricked them somehow? Blackmail? Or they had some sort of shared delusion?"

I shrug, wishing now I hadn't brought it up. Something about the atmosphere made it leap back into my mind, and I couldn't resist exorcising it, but I'm realizing now I have no idea how it ends. Did anyone ever figure out where she came from? What happened to her? "I don't know. They all really,

really believed she'd been with them from the start. Every one of them. It was like they all had false memories. My coworker told me they all kept saying, 'We've always known her. She's always been here.'"

They all just stare at me, obviously waiting for me to explain or say just kidding or something, but I shrug.

Logan repeats, "'We've always known her; she's always been here?' That's so creepy."

"Yeah. Sorry, shouldn't have started this vibe. Let's get back to lighter stuff."

At my side, Logan puts a hand on my knee and changes the subject, but I don't even hear what he says, because I'm frozen.

Allison, the other woman. She has braided pigtails.

Earlier she had one single braid.

I have two French braids, one sticking out from under my hat on each side.

Now she has two, one sticking out from under her hat on each side.

I'm speechless, the conversation casually continuing on among the three of them. I stare at her braids. I'm just—I'm sure of it. She had one, centered down her back.

I almost reach a hand up to touch mine, stop myself. I don't want to draw attention to it. When did she do that? Did she re-braid her hair while we were down at the creek? Or maybe when I was in the tent earlier? Why?

Logan is talking about our jobs now—they beat me to it after all—but I pick up my packet of chicken parm and start eating just so I don't have to talk for a minute, stalling to think. I burn my mouth.

Okay, maybe I'm overreacting. Is it really that weird?

It feels super fucking weird. Like, why do two? She'd seen me and my hair. Even if she just wanted to braid hers differently for some reason, why would she do what I have?

If it'd been me redoing my own, I intentionally would've chosen something different than the stranger I met, just to avoid the awkwardness of it seeming like I'd copied her.

Well, maybe she's less worried about seeming like a creeper than I am. Maybe she was ready for it to stop tickling the back of her neck and she just doesn't care if I think she's copying me.

I glance again, confirming.

She sees me look, smiles politely, then takes a bite of jerky, baring her teeth as she rips the chunk off.

A ripple of goose bumps trills up my spine. I fight the urge to visibly shiver with it, turning the spasm into a shift closer to the fire. I'm just unnerved because I told that stupid, weird story my coworker told me. It's probably not even true. She probably made it up or got it twisted. I've really hurt the roof of my mouth, and I've not even noticed the food I'm eating. I mechanically finish the packet, but the weird, artificial-tasting food is already turning into a heavy lump in my stomach.

From the corner of my eye, I study them, wondering if anything else has been changed. I can't point out anything specific, but then, we just met them. I might not even be able to pick them out of a lineup.

The darkness is full now, and one thing it does is desaturate all the colors. The trees look less green and more gray. The tents, two totally different colors, both look like obscure lumps off to each side. And her similar sweater, which was a lavender distinct from my powder blue one, could be any shade at all.

CHAPTER 6
LOGAN

They seem nice enough. Elise is being quiet now, but the other couple is just chatting and eating. After we've all finished our dinners, they bring out a partial bag of marshmallows and offer us some. I take two without hesitating. We almost packed some but decided we'd rather have the space, and on the first night Elise regretted it. We pop them on some long sticks to roast.

"Cheers," I say, holding up my 'mallow as if to toast.

"To new friends," Bryce says.

"And twinsies," Allison echoes, grinning. She dips hers forward as if to tap them like a glass, so we all swing ours in to the center, repeating, "Twinsies!"

Then there's the silence as we all find little pockets over the coals between flames to roast them. To my side, I sense Elise's stiffness. I think it's what we already talked about, but I can't help wondering if there's more. She wouldn't be weird about me accepting food from them, I don't think. It's not like they could've roofied a marshmallow. Maybe she's just irked that I accepted them because it extends the evening? Or maybe I underestimated how quickly she wanted to ditch them and head into the tent.

I put my hand on her knee, and she leans in. So. . . not mad at me. Even more uncomfortable with them?

I look at them across the fire, the orange flickering making their faces seem different. They're both gazing into the flames, concentrating on their skewers. They don't seem rude or weird or anything to me. Just a couple of backpackers like us hanging out.

A lot like us. It is actually kind of wild how much they look like us. We could be in one of those social media posts where people find unrelated near-identical strangers and have them take pictures together. I remember thinking Bryce was bigger than me, beefier, but sitting down low like he is and leaning, he seems even the same build as I am.

And Allison, who I initially thought was a less-beautiful version of Elise, is actually prettier than I thought. She doesn't have the same spirit, but I can imagine walking up to the wrong person if I saw her across a store or something.

I realize that she's watching me look at her. I drop my eyes to my marshmallow, pretending to examine it. I hope she doesn't think I was checking her out. I mean I was, but not that way.

"Kids?" she asks us.

It's the first thing anyone has said in a bit. The way she asks it, full of warmth and hope and commiseration and maybe even a little sorrow, it lands in the middle of the four of us like a flammable thing, right on the fire.

I feel shocked by it, even though it's the natural progression in the whole getting-to-know-you routine we've been enacting. Like a big raw wound she's poked with that skewer.

The moment seems too long. Eternity. We have to answer.

"Not yet," I say, at exactly the same time Elise says, "No."

The difference between our replies is stark. I actually close my eyes for a second, trying to absorb the hurt of us having to say it out loud.

From my side, where Elise is sitting up, shifting away from where she'd been leaning into me, I hear her force out the reciprocal, "You?"

CHAPTER 7
ELISE

I don't fully register their answer. It's some form of We're working on it, but beyond that I don't care. I just want to be done with this. With them.

They all look surprised to see me stand, and I realize I've done it abruptly, during something Bryce is saying. He's stopped, though, and they all stare at me, waiting for some explanation. The rustle of my wind jacket, added against the chill, seems loud.

I blink, smile sheepishly. "Nature calls." Then, on second thought, I turn to Logan. "Will you come with me?"

I know him so well that I see his bafflement, but they probably don't catch it. Maybe they think I'm needy or hapless. I don't care. Logan stands, popping his marshmallow into his mouth. "Sure. Time to turn in anyway. I need to go too."

I smile at the other couple, then point off behind our tent, opposite direction of theirs. "We'll find a spot off that way, and y'all can take that side? So, we don't have to worry about knocking," I joke.

They give polite smiles, nod. "No problem," Allison says, testing her burnt marshmallow with two fingers.

"It was so nice chatting with you two," Bryce says.

"Likewise," I parrot, and Logan gives a mouthful-mumble and a friendly wave of parting.

Then we toss our skewer sticks into the fire and I take his hand, guiding him out into the darkness of the woods beyond our tent. I consider stopping at the tent to grab the roll of toilet paper, but I have a pack of tissues in my pocket that will serve.

We don't talk. Eventually, I turn my headlamp back on, and Logan follows suit. I'm going farther than necessary. If Bryce and Allison were chatting, I'd wait until I couldn't hear them anymore, but since they're silent, I have to be sure they won't listen to anything we say. It's not weird for them to be silent at a campfire. Lots of people go silent, hypnotized by nature's TV. I try not to picture them staring at our backs the whole time we move into the trees.

In the dark, my atavistic brain tries to make every tall, slim shape into a person. Like a forest of creepers standing perfectly still, waiting to be seen before moving. Someone could be out here standing stock still, waiting, watching in plain sight. The eerie thing is how close I have to get to see what each shape actually is. Surprise: always a tree.

Eventually, as we're ducking under yet another yaupon branch in our way, Logan does speak up. "Are we just hiking back home tonight?" he asks, trying to sound playful. "Because I really like my backpack. The tent is whatever, but I'd like to bring the pack."

I try to smile at him, stopping. I cross my arms over my middle, cold even with the shell layer now that we're still and away from the fire. I can't even see it from here. More than enough privacy for peeing. "Maybe we should," I retort, and it doesn't sound playful.

"What's wrong?" he asks, and it's kind, not accusatory. But he clearly doesn't get it. Which is frustrating, because it means I'm the only one concerned here.

I take in a breath. "I just feel weird. They're off. It's strange how much they look like us. And Allison changed her hair."

He laughs, just one surprised scoff. "What?"

"She redid her braid, so she has two now."

I watch him look at my hair, where a braid drapes over my shoulders on each side. I brace myself for him to dismiss it, but he says, "She did?"

"Yeah."

"That. . . that is pretty weird. Yeah. I'm with you on that. But probably harmless?"

I nod, shrugging, shaking my head all in one confused spasm that morphs into a shiver. I step into Logan, prompting him to wrap his arms around me. "Probably," I say, dropping my forehead to his chest. I feel so tired, so worn down by everything. The weight of our struggles these past few years, the strain our indecision has put on our relationship, the way the whole damn world has seemed to spiral, and this trip. It just feels like such an insurmountable thing, to have the conversations we need to have here. And of course, now, with this other couple here tonight, we can't. I wish it felt like a reprieve, but it just feels like an extended deadline.

I let more of my weight lean into Logan, and he kisses the top of my head. "We really can go," he says. "I'll leave right now. I mean I would rather gather up our stuff, but if it's too awkward for you, I'll do it on my own and meet you up the trail."

The nuances of knowing someone like my own self. He means it. He would if I asked. But he also must know, speaking it out loud, how it sounds: drastic. And it's a small, but ongoing peeve of mine that he does this. I bring up a concern or idea, and he offers to act on it. Not actually acts on it but offers. The offer places the decision squarely on my shoulders and mine alone. In theory, it's a kindness. I get to enact my own preferences. But in reality, it's also a burden. If it's ultimately up to me, I'm responsible for whatever the outcomes are.

Is that fair? Maybe. Tonight at least, I am the one who's more worried, so maybe I should be the one to make the call. But it seems so extreme to leave now. I don't really want to be the one to inconvenience us that much. I'm also not crazy about the idea of walking in the dark when I already have the jitters.

I pull out of our embrace, looking for a stick to dig a little cathole divot for my eventual tissue after I pee. "No, it's okay. Let's just zip ourselves in and get through the night. At dawn we can skip breakfast and hit the trail."

"Okay," he says, walking a few trees away to relieve his bladder. "They're headed back to the trailhead, so come tomorrow we'll have the trip to ourselves again."

The relief I feel at the prospect is dampened by my unease. A night with them in our campsite. And then, once we're out, the dread of what's still left for us to decide.

CHAPTER 8
LOGAN

Thankfully, Bryce and Allison are gone when we get back into camp, so we don't have to do more pleasantries as we crawl into our tent. I briefly try to pick out if they're inside their own tent already, or maybe just off going to the bathroom like we were, but I don't hear or see any indications either way. They did put out the fire.

Elise is scared. Not just uncomfortable socially, but actually scared. I don't know if she realizes that, but she's not acting the way she acts at parties or when strangers try to talk to us out in public. She's acting the way she acts after she's stayed up watching a creepy movie. Staying close by me, huddling her body in on herself, eyes too wide. I keep thinking maybe I've missed something. Did one of them say something to her when I couldn't hear? She would've told me that; I'm almost certain.

As she's taking off her hiking boots to stash in the vestibule, I start unzipping both of our sleeping bags and zipping them to each other so they make one double-sized bag instead. It'll be less comfortable overall with the pads shifting around beneath us, but worth it, I think. She swivels her socked feet inside and zips the tent shut, then cocks her head to watch my ungraceful rearranging. When she realizes what I'm doing, her whole posture changes. Shoulders drop, face softening, big breath, small smile.

We work together to wrestle the bedding into order, which is easier said than done in a two-person tent and both of us in here, but we get it done. Then we shuck the outer layers of our clothes and climb in. I expect her to press her back into me, little spoon to my big spoon like we tend to favor at home, but instead she slides in facing me, so that we're hugging lying down.

Our "pillows" are lumpy bundles of clothes from our packs stuffed into the sleeping bag sacks. The pads under us aren't made to be side by side, so we're on a crack of overlap in the middle and gaps at the top and bottom. And the zipper is a rigid nuisance over my top shoulder. But our bodies are warm, and even though we smell like feet and pondwater and we never brushed our teeth before bed, it's Elise. It's her, and everything is okay for now.

She lifts her head, shifting, and does it several times so I realize she's bugged by her braids. She tries to reach up to undo one, but her elbows are in my face that way. "Let me?" I ask.

She nods, and I begin carefully unbraiding her hair. The outside of the sections is fuzzy and soft, but as I pull them apart, I feel that the inside is smooth and cool, maybe even still slightly damp. She tucks her forehead into my collarbone.

I speak without thinking, without overanalyzing it or wording it carefully. In a low, quiet voice that won't carry, I say, "I don't need kids to be happy. I want them, and I think it would be good, but I don't need them. But Elise? I do need you."

The sleeping bag rustles as she looks up at me. Her eyes are shiny in the dark. "I'm worried you're wrong." A loud swallow. "I'm worried you think that, but after years pass and it's too late, you'll look back and regret it. I'm scared you'll resent me."

I sigh. It reminds me of the way she won't just say, Let's leave now, and make the decision. Sometimes I wonder if she doesn't want to choose either way. She makes her opinion known, but not quite strongly enough to argue for it. She just wants to be able to speak up later and say she knew it. "I know you are," I say. "I'm scared too."

"What are you scared about?"

"That you'll feel pressured into having kids and then resent me."

She gives a choked little laugh. "We're a mess."

I've gotten both braids out. I pull her tighter, arms back under the sleeping bags. "If we don't both want it for sure, all the way, we shouldn't do it. I'd rather regret not having kids than regret having them."

I feel her shaking with silent crying. Relief? Disappointment? Overwhelm?

If we were home, maybe she'd let it all out, but here, I'm aware of the other couple within hearing range of anything louder than our murmurs. Elise grows still as she stifles whatever she's got going on, gets it reigned in. I don't know what this means. I don't know if she really knows what she wants. I'm not sure if she believes me, or if it's enough.

There's more to talk about, still a decision to be made. I don't know what the future is going to look like, but something in my chest eases a bit. I think, at least, that whatever it is, we'll deal with it together.

CHAPTER 9
ELISE

Logan's watch alarm is going off. I hear it distantly in my dream, am pulled to the surface by it. It's muffled. My arm is cold. I can't move my leg.

Finally, the beeping stops and he sits up, groaning. My leg is mobile again; his had been pinning it. One of my arms made its way out of the sleeping bag in the night, and my hand is frigid. I struggle to sit up, dragging my arm under the bag and pulling it up to my chin while my brain wakes up and everything comes back to me.

The tent, the smell of camping. Our issues, oof, our giant list of issues, and our talk last night. The skinny dipping. The other couple.

"The other couple," I whisper, and I'm on my knees, putting my outer layers back on and beginning to pack up our stuff. It's before dawn. Logan set his alarm for fifteen minutes before so we could be walking out of here as soon as there's light, before the other couple wakes up. Hopefully Logan's watch wasn't too loud. I don't think it was.

We move as quickly as we can while still minimizing noise, but it's not silent. Nylon is noisy. I leave off my wind jacket, but still, everything inside a tent is whistly and rustley and zippy. There's the whisper of fabric on fabric as we stuff the sleeping bags into their cases, the hiss of air as we open the valves on the sleeping pads and lay on top of them to squeeze out the inflation. Then there's the extended squeal of the main door, and our boots crunching on the ground.

I look to their tent and see no movement, hear nothing. Hopefully they're heavy sleepers. But standing has made me realize that I'm going to need to go before we go. "I have to go to the bathroom," I whisper.

Logan glances at me, out to where we walked last night, and then again at the other tent. "Okay," he whispers back, hesitating. I can see him predicting my train of thought, my worst- case scenario. What if they wake up and see us leaving? How awkward would that be? "I'll take down the tent." When I hesitate, he adds, "There's nothing wrong with getting an early start."

I cringe a bit, but he's right, and I don't have much choice. I grab the roll of toilet paper and head off to get some privacy.

My headlamp illuminates my path through the woods, and I'm forced to slow enough to dodge spiderwebs and avoid being scraped in the face by branches. It takes me a minute to realize I'm cold. I have my beanie on, and my hair is down now, offering some coverage to my neck, but it got chilly overnight.

When I have enough privacy that I know I won't get stumbled on if the other folks start milling about, I do my business. The odd, detached feeling of squatting in the dark, my light putting a circle of ground in front of me in high relief, the rest of me blind to myself. I finish as quickly as I can, listening for I don't know what, but I hear only night forest sounds. Wind, frogs, crickets. One shrill, distant bird.

When I've covered over my cathole and straightened my clothes, I tuck the roll of toilet paper under my arm and head back to camp.

With no campfire to guide me, it's dicier. For a moment, I wonder if I've gotten myself turned around, but a flash of headlamp guides me into the opening of the campsite.

It looks odd with our tent down. I'd hoped it would be packed already—Logan's pretty quick at it—but it's still spread collapsed on the earth like a fallen parachute. I scan for a figure, Logan's form squatting to pull up the stakes or standing by a tree to pee, but there's no one by the tent or even off behind it.

Then a light draws my head across to the other side of camp. To their side.

A figure stands there.

No, two figures. The other couple is up?

Lights shine directly at me as heads swivel to illuminate me.

It's three lights. Three figures.

"Logan?" I ask, as if anyone else might be here. It's still dark, dawn in the process of breaking, and with the three head lamps all aimed directly at me, I can't see any of their faces.

"Yeah," comes a voice, and I swear it's echoed, doubled. Did Bryce just answer at the same time?

One of the figures steps away from the other two, then another one, so that they're spaced out better. The lights still obscure faces. I can tell from the height that the person on the far right is Allison—her arms are lifted, doing something to her hair—but Logan and Bryce look the same in their layers, in the dark.

I raise a hand to shield my eyes from their light beams, both trained on me. Why did Logan go over to talk to them? Did they wake up and need help with something? I really wanted us to be out of here before talking to them again.

"Elise," Logan says, but he doesn't come toward me.

I stand awkwardly, wishing they'd freaking turn off their headlamps, but then I realize I'm blinding them too, trying to pick out Logan, so I turn mine off and head over toward our tent so he can follow me over.

For some reason, even after I make it to our tent, he doesn't.

The three of them stand there staring at me for a minute, and I don't know what to say. Finally, Logan says again, "Elise."

Bryce says it right after, but he sounds so much like Logan that I wonder if it was Bryce who said it first. It's weird, in the dark, Logan at their tent. One of the guys starts walking toward me, and I don't like how I can't tell which one it is.

Then the other one does too, and even Allison.

"What's going on?" I say, stepping back. "Will y'all turn off your lights?" I add, hand up to shield my eyes.

One of them turns off his light. I squint, my eyes adjusting in blooms of yellow as I try to tell who it is.

Logan.

He's almost to me, and the relief I feel is palpable, tangible, an actual release of weight on my chest. I suck in a big breath, about to sigh and reach for him, when Bryce turns his light off too. I glance at him, then freeze, a hand hovering in the air where I was reaching toward Logan.

Because it's not Bryce. It's Logan.

I jerk my hand back, realizing I was reaching for Bryce accidentally. My cheeks flush hot, and I glance at him, already turning my body toward the real Logan.

But it's Logan.

A bizarre clump of a word that didn't form drops from my lips, a puppy-like mewl of confusion and startle.

Both of the men stop a couple yards away, looking at me. I clench my eyes shut, shake my head rapidly, as if I can shake out the stars marring my vision. It's screwing me up, the headlamps. I really thought they both looked like Logan. Not in the way that Bryce had looked like him last night that we'd all talked about, but actually. I'd been certain, twice, that I saw Logan.

I open my eyes, looking again. My vision has cleared. It's dark, the dim of predawn, but not so dark that I can't see their faces.

They both look like Logan.

I feel myself scowl. My confusion is so deep it feels like anger. "What?" I snap. "What's—"

Logan says, "Elise, I don't—"

He's interrupted by Logan: "Babe, there's something—"

They both sound like him. They both look like him. My mouth is open on a dangling question that dried up on my tongue. I glance behind them to Allison, as if she'll be able to give this any type of fathomable answer, and she's staring at me with a surprisingly neutral expression.

On my face.

CHAPTER 10
LOGAN

I watch Elise see that Allison looks like her, and I try to think of what to say. What do I say? The only things I can think of are shellshocked questions and idiotically obvious statements. How is this happening?

What is happening?

Then, before I can formulate anything at all, Allison runs at Elise.

And I mean runs.

"Don't!" I yell.

Bryce, in my voice, shouts, "Stop!"

"Run," I tell Elise, but she's just beginning to turn when Allison tackles her.

The other woman catches Elise by the side, smacking into her shoulder and spinning my wife as they fall. Her hair billows out the bottom of her hat; I think she's unbraided it.

"Hey," I shout. As I lurch forward to pull her off my wife, I'm slammed forward.

I fall to the ground, chin hitting dirt. Bryce has tackled me. I wasn't braced for it. I was in motion, didn't have a good stance.

He falls on top of me, gripping my shoulders and rolling. I don't even have time to fight back before he shouts, "Get off me!" Then he scuttles back and away, as if I've attacked him.

"I wasn't on you," I say, baffled, angry, turning to Elise. I need to get Allison off her.

They're scrambling away from each other, each looking equally horrified.

Each looking equally like my wife.

"What the fuck," Elise breathes, panting.

Across from her, edging away from Bryce, who looks like me, Elise says, "Oh my God. I don't—what the—"

The other Elise finishes, "Oh my God."

Whatever this is, whoever they are, in a matter of moments they've made it impossible for me to tell which Elise is the real one. And as they both look from me to Bryce and back, what seems genuine fear and confusion on both faces, I realize they've done the same with me for Elise.

One of those women who look like Elise is Elise, but who is the other?

CHAPTER 11
ELISE

The four of us have all backed away from each other, like we're tucked in the corners of an invisible boxing ring. We're all on the ground, spaced almost equally apart. I don't want to touch any of them until I know which one is Logan—the real Logan. I guess he feels the same. And the other two?

I guess they're pretending to feel the same.

"What's going on here?" I mutter, mind racing. The explanations I come up with are rapid, under-formed. A reality TV show or internet video. Some freaky-good prosthetic masks and body doubles. Or deepfake technology somehow projected in real time. There's no one filming though. No crew, no phones out.

I pat my pocket at the thought of my phone, but I don't have it. We always shut them off and put them in our packs when we go hiking. What's the point of being in nature if you're looking at it through your screen the whole time? But now it's out of reach, off, closer to her than me. I think about running for it, but I'm afraid of giving her the idea.

It could be a hallucination. Maybe I've had some sort of mental break and I'm just imagining they look like us. But no, because Logan sees it too, whichever one of them he is. I look back and forth between the two Logans, and I truly, seriously cannot tell which one he is. I lock eyes with one of them, and the feeling I get is the one I get when I look into Logan's eyes. Maybe it's him. I look at the other, and I feel it again too. They both seem real. They both feel real.

My heart hurts in my chest. Clenches at the fear I feel. Never in all my life with him, together since we were teens, did I dream I would be afraid when I looked into his eyes.

The word clone leaps to my attention, my brain desperately trying to find some answer. But clones aren't real, not this way. They have to grow. And who would clone both of us? And why?

A glitch in the matrix, or some form of it. Like a creator messed up. But no, because we weren't just instantaneously and spontaneously duplicated. There were other people here first. They looked a lot like us, but they weren't us. They were Allison and Bryce—or pretending to be—but they've somehow changed.

Androids. A cyborg type facsimile. Some intensely advanced technology that could recreate us so faithfully that I can't even tell it's a machine. But I've seen the internet videos of our most advanced robots, and we are not even close to being this good. I'm looking into either Logan or Bryce's eyes, and they sure as hell seem sentient.

So, what? Aliens? Demons? Monsters?

My heart is pounding, because I thought she was attacking

me. Allison. Well, she did, but I mean really attacking. I thought she was trying to hurt me, kill me. Instead, she just mixed us up and backed away. That's almost worse. If she'd tried to kill me, I could've fought back. But this?

If I try to hurt her, Logan might think I'm her and try to hurt me to stop it.

And I don't know if that's even what I want. Should I try to hurt her? Is she going to try to hurt me? Why are they doing this?

My head hurts. I take a deep breath, and it shudders. "Logan," I say, testing it.

They both look to me. No hesitation.

"I'm Elise," I say.

"I'm the real Elise," 'Allison' protests, her voice sounding so scared it cracks.

The notion of her using fake fear to make her sound sympathetic pisses me off. "I can prove it," I say, trying to level my own voice. "I'm me. Ask me anything I'd know and I'll prove it."

But of course, I don't know which Logan I'm talking to.

There's a long pause as they both stare at me, thinking, and then the one across from me says, "What's our address?"

"2905 Orchid Street," I say, at the same time that Allison says it.

CHAPTER 12
LOGAN

The Elise across from me whispers, "Stalkers."

The Elise to my left says, "She repeated me! She said it right after I did!"

"I did not," the one across from me snaps. "We said it at the same time."

"Okay, let's just—hold on," says Bryce, sitting to my right. "We can do it one at a time."

It seriously pisses me off that he sounds exactly like me. Not an impression of me, but actually me.

"You," he says, pointing at the Elise across from me. "Only you answer this one. What's our cat's name?"

I think because he knows what this is—whatever the actual fuck this is—he's a step ahead of me. He's not as shocked as me, so he can think of what the smart thing to say would be and say it first. I'm worried it makes me look like the fake Logan, like I'm not as eager to prove who's who.

Elise says, "We have two. Holly and Doc."

God, it sounds like her. "Why?" I challenge.

She looks at me. "For Tombstone. After Doc Holliday."

That's right. The tightness squeezing my chest loosens. I hold her gaze, try to mentally send her my thoughts. It's me, I'm the real me. I think you're you. She looks at me with wide eyes, deep frown lines on her forehead. Does she see me? Does she know me?

Bryce looks at the Elise to my left and asks, "What was the first thing I said to you?"

I glance at her. There's no way she could know that.

"Fluffy," she says softly. "You were in the seat behind me. You petted my hair and said, fluffy."

Fire surges up my throat. Because she's right. And she's saying it not to me, but to him.

So, the one across from me might not be the real Elise. How could the fake one know that? Either of those things?

It's possible that they researched us online. I almost never post anything, but Elise does sometimes. She's definitely put pictures of the cats on social media. Would she have said why we named them Holly and Doc? Maybe, but that would mean these people targeted us, researched us deeply, and then pretended to run into us. Even if they did, they still somehow changed to look identical. No matter how I look at that, it's paranormal. They might even know what we know.

Instead of raising another question, I think about physical things. Their clothes were different than ours too. Similar, but not the same.

Dawn is lifting the darkness. It's bright enough now that my headlamp skews tone more than actually making things easier to see, so I reach up and turn it off. After a second, everyone else does too. Copying, or just realizing what I've realized? I study the jackets on both Elises. They were both light colors, but not the same. I can't remember what anymore, but now they're both light blue. Same zip, collar, brand logo. Same jacket. Same shirt under, same boots, same pants. Everything is a perfect match.

Did they meet us looking different to ease us close, or did they need time to assimilate?

"What's in your pants pocket?" I ask, looking at both Elises. I really hate that I'm thinking of them that way. I try to mentally correct myself to Elise and "Allison," but since I don't know which is Allison, I can't make my mind keep using that.

The Elise across from me says, "Tissues! A packet of tissues!" kind of excitedly, like she's happy to prove herself.

Glancing at her, the Elise to my left straightens her leg out so she can reach into her pocket. She digs in and comes out with a packet of travel tissues. She holds it up between two fingers like a prize.

We all look to the Elise across from me. She's got her own leg straightened out so she can reach into her pocket. She frowns, leans further back, and digs into the other one. When she comes up with nothing, she switches back to the first, then stands up, searching her back pockets. "I know I had them," she mutters, face flushing coral. "I have them."

She pats her fleece, digs into its front pockets, but she comes up with nothing. We're all three looking up at her as she looks down at the Elise to my left. "Did you steal my tissues?" she asks, more baffled than accusatory.

The look on Elise's face, to my left, is pure Elise. It's like an eyeroll without rolling her eyes. It's so perfectly her, that I know. It's her. She has the pack of tissues. She knew how we met. She has the right facial expressions.

That's Elise.

CHAPTER 13
ELISE

Now I'm the only one who's gotten a question wrong.

I don't know where my pack of tissues is. I always stick it in my pocket. Did Allison take it during the scuffle? It doesn't seem like she had time for that. And why would she?

If she's so powerful that she can transmute something from my pocket into hers, why bother planting tissues and pretending to be me?

Why are they both pretending to be us?

If they wanted to replace us, they could've just killed us. They've had plenty of opportunities. Even if she didn't dematerialize my pack of tissues, they still could've snuck up on us while we were sleeping. So, they don't want to kill us, and they don't want to replace us. Or at least, not both of us.

Just one?

Why?

Infiltration.

I'm the only one standing, and all three of them look up at

me. Logan, Logan, and me. A ripple of goosebumps rises so noticeably up my neck that I cringe into it, shuddering.

I don't know which one of them is really Logan, but I'm betting he now thinks I'm not me. It's what I would think if I were him. What are we going to do?

What if he leaves without me?

My throat tightens, hot under my jaw at the thought of being left behind. What if she—it?—"Allison" tricks him and they leave me here with Bryce? What if Logan is fully duped, and just. . . goes home with her? Lives with her?

What would "Bryce" do if I'm stuck out here with him, stranded?

Kill me?

My breath is coming fast, noticeable in our silence. No one seems to know what to do.

"We have to go," I say without thinking. It comes out too loud, and one of the Logans twitches. "We have to get out of here." Of course, what I mean is we double, not quadruple. If only I knew which one of them was the one I wanted to take home.

It occurs to me that I haven't asked them any questions. I answered the one they lobbed at me, but I didn't return any. I haven't tried to catch one of them in a lack of knowledge.

But Allison knew how we met. She knew that the first thing Logan ever said to me was "fluffy," sitting behind me in freshman lit class and petting my frizzy hair like I was a soft cat. I thought he was weird as fuck, doing that. Uninvited touch? No thank you. We were teenagers, but still. It's not my favorite meet-cute, not a story I've told people or shared broadly. There's no way she could know that unless she knows what I know. Everything I know.

And if they know what we know, somehow searching the databases of our memories on demand, quizzing them isn't going to tell me which one is the real Logan.

I'm left with something deeper, more inherent than quizzing. Mannerisms, habits, but even more. Just. . . essence. Which one of these Logan acts and seems and feels like my Logan?

"Logan," I say, and they both look alert. It was worth a try. "We need to get away, get somewhere safe."

Maybe I should've run when I had the chance. Maybe I should've just fucking bolted back toward the trailhead as fast as I can. But the trailhead is three full days' hike away. Even running, I couldn't do it in a single stretch of daylight. They would be able to catch up to me at some point, maybe, and I wouldn't be able to control which one of them it was. A footrace isn't the right way to determine who's who. And even if I managed to get back to the car first, what was I going to do? Leave?

Without Logan?

No. Besides—

"The keys are in our stuff," says the Logan across from me.

We all four look at the collapsed tent, spread on the ground in the dawn dim, a small mound beside it that must be our backpacks.

Logan, the one beside me, launches himself off the ground, running toward the tent. The other Logan, across from me, yells, "Hey!" and follows.

The first one skids to a stop practically on top of the packs, grabbing at the zipper. The second one slams into him, knocking him onto his side as he grabs for the pack. My jaw is hanging open.

Allison jolts to her feet. She yells, "Stop. Stop! Both of you, stop!" and her tone is so frightened and emotional that the Logan currently unzipping the pack freezes. The other Logan sits up, shoves him, hard, but stills after. They both look at her.

They think she's me. Logan for sure thinks she's the real me, because of course he wouldn't stop for her.

Does that mean the first Logan, who stopped first, is the real one?

I want to screech at her: Stop using my voice! Instead, I suck in a huge breath and try to sound calm. "She's right. Y'all fighting isn't going to make anything better. Neither of you can take the keys until we figure this out."

"I'll take them," Allison says, stepping forward with some authority.

I scoff. "Why would we let you take them? No way."

She frowns at me. "Well, you can't have them either."

I sigh, filling both cheeks and funneling the air through pursed lips, and I see the first Logan notice, cock his head. Recognize my gesture? Doubt his assessment of Allison as me? Recognition, the first one to think of the keys, the first one to run for them, and the first one to stop when she yelled it. I mentally tag him as maybe the real Logan.

"Okay," I say, tone forced steady. "Let's all be reasonable. None of us is going to be okay with any of the others taking the car keys.

I don't think fighting over them is going to make anyone more confident." I send a vaguely accusatory look at Logan, and my whole world threatens to spill into nonsense as I have to double it. I swallow, force my gaze away from them. "We need a plan for how to get back to the car."

Logan—the first one who I'm thinking is the real one—says, "We can't go back to the car."

My eyes go wide, but before I can respond, Allison says, "What do you mean? We have to go back!"

I narrow my eyes at her. I can't believe how angry I am. Her using "me" to act not quite how I would is infuriating. By the time I realize that's pretty much my response too, Logan answers.

"There are four of us. Two of you," he says, and I hear anger in his voice too, and I don't like that it's partially directed at me, "can't go back with us. We can't allow it. No one goes back to the car until we know it's the right two."

"That's—that's actually what I was going to say," says the other Logan, and he sounds so reluctant to admit it that I question my leaning toward the first one as the real one. "Only the right two can take the car, and since we all disagree right now, no one gets to take the keys."

"I kind of agree," Allison admits.

My pulse is right under my ears, hot like rising mercury. I'm so mad I can hardly see straight. Dawn is rising and the woods are brightening imperceptibly, and I am the odd one out. Somehow, both Logan and the other Logan and Allison all agree—against me.

CHAPTER 14
LOGAN

I've done the math, and the worst thing I can imagine happening is that the real Elise goes back home with the fake me, believing he's really me. It's not even about what would happen to me. Allison could kill me or abandon me; the scariest thought is that Elise might just go on living her life as if I were still with her. To be replaced might be the worst thing I can think of. And to what end? What insidious purpose?

So yeah, I'm not letting us go to the car to hash this out. Get close enough for one of them to make a move and take off? No way.

I think about going for my cell phone, but I know that Bryce will want it too, because he'll have to pretend it's his, and only one of us can get it. The phone is like the car; getting us closer to aid also gets them closer to aid.

I'm not wild about the idea of sitting around this campsite arguing, either. Just, what, sharing meals and trying to keep an eye on them all so no one jumps me or steals the keys and makes a run for it? Continue playing Double Jeopardy? And what if we're here all day without any change? We're going to camp again? With who in which tent? The idea of sharing a tent with the Elise who might be the fake Elise makes my heart hurt, and the idea of sharing one with Bryce makes my skin run cold. And any combination that might involve Elise in a tent with either of them, me separated with no way to know if she's safe: no.

Maybe I pull Bryce aside, talk to him one-on-one. Maybe if it's just us two, he'll stop pretending to be me and I can try to figure out what he actually wants. But, again, that would put Elise alone with Allison, and since we don't know what they want, I can't tolerate that. I won't turn my back or walk away long enough to risk her doing something to the real Elise.

There's only one better option that I can come up with, and since no one else is volunteering solutions, I pitch it. "I think we should keep hiking."

I watch the Elises' reactions.

The Elise I think is the fake one looks so confused it borders on angry. The Elise I think is the real one lets her mouth drop open, snaps it shut, and almost smiles for a second, like she thinks I'm joking or knows something I don't. Neither reaction tells me much more or changes my mind, which is what I'm hoping for at this point. Catching them out somehow. Confirming to myself which is which so I can take some kind of action. It's just… the cost of being wrong is so high.

I swallow, finally looking to Bryce. His face is still, guarded. I don't know what he thinks of my suggestion. It's a strange feeling, to want to attack someone who looks just like me. I've had my moments of looking in the mirror and not loving what I see, but I've never wanted to physically hurt myself before. Of course, he's not me. That's the mindfuck. He's an imposter, and I want so badly to knock him unconscious. Maybe even kill him. I thought about it, but I'm afraid that it'll make the real Elise think I'm him. She's never seen me be aggressive, because I've never had to be in front of her before. Not really.

Not to mention that it would be an incredibly well-balanced fight. He seems to know at least what I know, and probably more. Physically, could I take myself out? Even with the element of surprise, I'm not sure.

Finally, the Elise I think is the fake one says, "Why on Earth would we keep hiking?"

"What else are we going to do?" I counter. "We're not going back to the car where someone can try to make a break for it, and there's no reason to stay here."

The other Elise interrupts, "Well all of our stuff is here. . ." She trails off as she realizes the issue. Whose stuff, exactly? And how would we divvy that up? No one will want to claim the other tent and supplies.

Bryce says, "Keep going up trail for how far? Until what?"

I swallow, something big and heavy sinking in my guts, some sense of finality I can't articulate. "Until we figure this out," I answer with more certainty in my tone than I really feel.

They have to know what that implies. Something final. Something certain.

Something irreversible.

CHAPTER 15
ELISE

I think it's Bryce trying to get us to keep hiking.

Logan isn't this decisive. Never has been. I can't imagine him pushing for this when I've said I want to do the opposite.

Then again, he probably doesn't think I'm really me. Maybe he's doing the opposite because he thinks I'm Allison trying to trick them into going to the cars?

I still don't think he'd be this sure, this insistent.

I think he's Bryce.

But I can't, for the life of me, think of a way to convince them all to change their minds. If Logan and I had each other with certainty and could step aside to discuss, we could come up with something. But this, this not being sure who's who, it makes it three against one. Or at least one against one against two.

Do they have a way to keep track of each other?

Because Logan and I, no matter which one he really is, are divided.

The thought of something happening to him is the worst thing

I've ever imagined. Us being separated forever, however, makes one thing abruptly and excruciatingly clear: I want to stay together. I don't want to get a divorce. I don't want to "set him free" and let him go marry someone else who definitely wants kids. I want him. I want Logan. Forever, together, just like we vowed.

And yeah, maybe I don't want kids. Maybe I would've, if things were different than they are, but they're not, and I think it's time for me to admit to myself and to Logan that I'm allowed to change my mind. I'm allowed to want what I want, and I don't want to be a mother.

He told me that he can be happy with that. With me. With just me.

I need to let myself believe him.

If only I can figure out which one is him.

CHAPTER 16
LOGAN

Hiking without a backpack on feels wrong, like I'm constantly forgetting something. It's so much easier, after days of lugging the big pack around, that I feel supercharged. Or maybe that's the adrenaline.

One of the Elises suggested we grab the packs, but there was immediate argument over who would get them, because, of course no one would claim the others' gear—and I wasn't willing to let anyone but me have access to the phones and/or car keys—so we left them at camp. It felt vaguely reassuring, like I'd be back soon just by leaving them there. Sure, Logan. That's how it works.

The morning is misty, saturating the air so it smells of wet vegetation and damp rocks. The trail here is shadowed by trees, the sun not breaking through yet, so that it looks like we're entering a gray tunnel.

There's a moment when we all start walking up the trail that I feel like I'm genuinely losing my mind. It's just so surreal how casual it feels on the surface. If the others didn't look exactly like us, it could be two couples going on a hike.

We sort of naturally funnel onto the trail, side by side. The other couple is in front. The Elise beside me is the one I think is fake, but even so, her being at my side is so deeply normal, so emotionally ingrained, that I almost reach out and take her hand. It would be so nice to have that right now. Being able to hold hands is definitely something I've taken for granted. I glance to see that she's reaching for my hand too, whether because she saw me start the gesture out of habit, or because she also wanted to.

We see each other's hands drifting toward each other, jerk them back, look at each other's faces, eyes wide. I almost say, Sorry, as if I've reached for a stranger's hand by mistake, which maybe I have, but if that's what I've done, it's presumably what the stranger wanted me to do.

She makes a little muffled, surprised upset sound, lifting her hands to adjust her hat, as if I were a date that got uninvitedly frisky and she had to subtly keep it out of reach from now on. She is wearing Elise's outdoor ring, but so is the other Elise. Bryce too, has a ring like mine.

I stop walking, which lets her shift to the center of the trail and relieves us from hiking side by side. Am I wrong about her being the fake Elise?

Wouldn't the fake one want me to buy in as her being the real one, and take my hand?

The real one might be as doubtful as me, and unwilling to risk taking the wrong hand.

Unless the fake one is so on the ball that she knew that's how it would seem and pretended to be put off by us almost holding hands.

I close my eyes for a moment. I feel sick.

Then my eyes flash open because I realize I can't look away for long. They could mix us up again. Not that I'm certain who's who—eighty percent sure is not enough when it comes to identifying my wife—but I don't need it to be even harder. I can't let them out of my sight.

It makes me glad I've ended up at the back of the line, even if the others keep glancing back at me. They're probably worried I'm going to turn and make a break for it, but unlike the probably-fake Elise who suggested going back to the cars, I'm not trying to get out of here. Not without Elise.

I'm not crazy about not being able to see where we're going, but I'd rather that than not being able to see who's right behind me. If I remember right, the next landmark on this trail is a vista. Rocky Ridge, or something like that.

Bryce has taken the lead, leaving Elise and Allison in the middle.

We hike in silence until the morning has worn on, the sun finally cresting the treetops to give us proper light, and a glimmer of warmth sinks into my clothes. I begin to get hungry—no breakfast—but we didn't bring our food because we couldn't agree who'd go through which packs to carry what. Every choice feels loaded, not just because my mind is warning DANGER, but because I feel myself being assessed, judged. Every movement and word evaluated. It makes me second-guess everything.

At the same time, I'm trying to do that to the two Elises. I'm hyper-focused on how I'm coming across while also trying to analyze each step and facial twitch and word that comes from both of them.

And what are we going to do when we get to the end of the trail?

We've been ascending rocky hills for a while now, mostly in quiet, for long enough that my already-sore legs are burning. The Elise in front of me has been slowing down, gradually, but progressively, to the point that I finally say, "Pick up the pace."

Bryce pauses where he's gained a good ten yards' lead, and the Elise behind him, who I think is the real Elise, looks a question at us.

"I think they're trying to split us up," I tell her. "We need to stay together."

She stares me in the eyes, and I realize I've shown my hand by saying they about the other two. Now she knows I think she's the real Elise. Well, good. Maybe. Maybe that will help her see I'm me.

My heart is pounding as I wait for her to react.

CHAPTER 17
ELISE

The Logan who I think is Bryce has just said they about me and the real Logan.

Why would the two imposters want to stay together? If they're trying to be convincing to us, they can't both do it. If they have me and Logan split up, they can convince one of us.

It's the first time I've thought of it that way. Maybe they're not trying to convince both of us together.

Maybe they're trying to convince each of us separately.

It could be that they don't want to replace us both. They want to replace one of us.

If that's the case, the other two, whoever, whatever they are, aren't both trying to go home instead of both of us. They're trying to swap one of us out to go home with the real remainder. One of us replaced within each "couple." Separated. Deceived.

I watch Allison, in my identical body, react to Bryce revealing who he thinks is the real us. Her lips part in surprise, then her hands float forward as if unintentionally to reach for his before she snatches them back, stopping herself. Her eyes are full of unspilled emotion.

She's really fucking good.

His face too, is vivid with micro emotions, a full gamut of feelings restrained. His eyebrows leap in hope. His body leans forward, as if to take her hands, until she pulls them back. He drops his own, jaw tight, brows dipping, face schooled.

Is it Bryce? Is he that good? Or am I wrong?

I look around her, up ahead to the lead Logan—the one I've been thinking might be the real Logan. I expect him to be watching them too, analyzing like I am, but he's looking at me. I almost startle at how directly he's staring at me. It gives me the impression he's been staring at me, watching me for a while. My breath is coming fast, short unsatisfying inhales. Is he Logan? What has he seen, watching me watch them? Have I acted the way I'm supposed to? The way he'd believe I would?

Before I can second guess myself, I'm walking past Allison to get to the lead Logan. His eyes widen in surprise.

The others stand still as I go, until I'm beside him. The one who is, I think, the real Logan. And if the other two think they've found each other, I suppose us two pairing up for now is what's left. I don't take his hand, don't say anything, but it feels clear to me.

They both follow my lead, moving side by side.

I'll walk with him. They'll walk with each other. And those of us who want to know will see if we can determine who's correct.

CHAPTER 18
LOGAN

The day is warming up. There's less tree cover around, which gives me glimpses of broad views. The mist has evaporated, and we've climbed high enough that the earth smells different. Now the rocks smell arid, and the plants smell like dry grass and pollen. It's late morning, close to the early lunch we'd usually stop for on a full backpacking day. My stomach is telling me we skipped breakfast.

The angle of the rise we're hiking up makes me think we're close to the overlook. I've never been on this trail before, so I don't know what it looks like, but I've been on enough hikes to sense that this incline can't sustain itself much longer. Not around here, anyway. The "peaks" of the Arbuckle Mountains in this part of Oklahoma just aren't that dramatic. We're going to rise to the top of something.

Elise and I are in the back, a couple yards behind Allison and Bryce. No one has spoken in several minutes. No one touches, which also tells me I'm not the only one less than one hundred percent confident I'm right about who's who.

I find myself analyzing our clothes.

I keep thinking that they can't be perfect recreations of us. It's just so hard to believe that anyone, anything, could replicate so precisely. The two Elises, so far, have checked out, though. Their boot laces, peeking under the bottoms of their gray pants, are dark green with little lighter specks. The rubber sole on the side of the right boot has a split in it. The pants have a cargo pocket on only the left leg. The butt has a little metal brand logo. The fleece quarter-zip pills ever so slightly on the sides, where the arms have rubbed while they walk. Their hair is down, growing into a big cloud of curls that poufs from under the bright orange hats.

Their skin, the bit that shows, is identical too. I check freckles, cuticles, nail length. I can't find a single discrepancy, no matter how small.

So, I study Bryce. It's weird, because I never see myself from the back. Elise's butt? Like the back of my hand. But mine? Only in pictures. I'm not thrilled with the way my side fat sticks out at the top of my pants, but that's a problem for another day.

What I do know is my gear. He's got my same mid-high-top boots with the sole flap on the left foot. The same campfire ember scorch on the lower left pant leg. The quarter zip, frayed along the bottom hem, that's just slightly too tight, but not tight enough to replace it yet. He even has his sleeves pushed up to his elbows like I do. On his wrist, same digital watch with a black paracord strap, made out of that braided survival rope for worst case scenarios. Green hat, no brand visible. As far as I can tell, he's identical to me.

And he seems to know what I know too. Or at least he has access to my memories. Can he read my mind now?

I stare at him, waiting to see if he'll glance back at me, but he doesn't. Because he can't "hear" me thinking about him, or because he knows I'm waiting to see if he will and he doesn't want me to know?

They've already proven they can access our memories. If they can also read our minds now, in real time as we think things, we're fucked. I don't think there's any besting that. I'd like to believe it's just memories in a big database they have to thumb through, not current thoughts. Not actually inhabiting our minds. Because I have a plan developing, and if they know what I'm thinking as I think it, it won't work.

I need to believe it might work.

CHAPTER 19
ELISE

We're coming up to the top of a rise. I never noticed when exactly the sound of the creek dropped away, but it has, far below us and barely audible. Mostly now I hear birds, insects, wind, and my heartbeat drumming in my ears. The birds have morphed from the small noisy friends of the forest to faraway, feral cries from sky seekers.

We've been in and out of shade, and there's still scrub brush on both sides of the trail, but we're coming up to an area ahead where there are no trees. I think it's a plateau at the top of a cliff.

I do not want to be near a cliff right now.

I imagine the drop, can't quite see it yet, but I can see enough around us—out and over the scrub to how large the gap is, how far out of sight any ground is—to intuit that it's a deadly fall. Or at least a body-breaking fall. Whatever the edge is, it's one that, once crossed, you're falling all the way down, not stopping yourself.

What if they push us?

The possibilities are numerous. Logan, the Logan I think is

really Logan, walks beside me, but does he really believe I'm me? If he thinks I'm not, would he try to shove me off?

Bryce and Allison, I think, are behind us. Would she push me? Or him? What if I'm wrong, and that's the real Logan? He could push her. Or me. It's just so risky.

It was Bryce's idea, I think, to keep going. He said it was because we couldn't let the other two take the keys or go back to the car, but what if it was actually so we'd all be up there together, four of us stranded at the top of this rise?

We're in the lead, me and Logan. If we're going to do something, we need to decide it now. Even as I think I can see the trail flattening out ahead. We're almost there.

I could push them.

The thought slices me like a knife. Unbidden. Unwelcome.

But true.

I could. I really could. I don't have to wait to see if they're going to try to push me or not. I might not feel confident enough to push Bryce, but I damn well know which one is Allison.

I could shove her over the edge.

A million variations ripple through my imagination. I see her grabbing my arms as I push, watching my own shocked expression as she pulls me down with her. I see Bryce sneak up on Logan and shove him while I shove her, so that they both fall and I'm left with him, by myself, no real Logan to help me. I see trying, failing: Logan thinking I never would've done that—Logan confirming that I'm not really me, even though I am, and never believing me again. I see succeeding, shoving her, somehow shoving

Bryce, being okay, going home, having to live with the memory of murdering two people for the rest of my life.

All of them in an instant. None of them okay.

But what else is there?

I could turn and run. A bit late to try it, maybe, but if I'm lucky, not too late. I could sprint downhill right past the other two and not stop until I either get to the campsite to grab the keys or until someone catches me. But again, I'm left with the absolute terror of Logan thinking I'm not me because of whatever I choose. I'm not just choosing what I think is best; I need to choose what I think he'd think I'd choose.

Besides, whatever I do, it can't end with me leaving here alone. I can't just leave the real Logan behind with these two. I don't know what they want, what they are, or what they'd do to him. I'd never forgive myself.

I could just tell everyone to stop. Right now. No one goes up there. We. . . what? Sit down and talk this out? Try the quizzing again? Go back to camp? Play rock paper scissors?

We're almost to the top. I'm out of time to come up with ideas. I have to make a decision, and the repercussions of literally every decision I can think of are so huge, so unbearable if I'm wrong, that I feel incapacitated.

I don't know what to do.

I don't want this. I don't want the weight of this all on me.

My legs have kept going as I panic. I see the area spread out before us as we crest the trail. It's a large, open plateau of shallowly-soiled rock, no plants growing despite ample sun, spilling into a beautiful scenic overlook at the precipice of a rocky cliff. The vista on the map for sure. There's more of the rocky wall to the left, where the mountain peaks a bit above us, but the front and right sides form an almost one-hundred-and-eighty-degree view. No railing.

I've broken into a sweat. I should've taken off my fleece sweater at some point during the hike, but I was too focused on other things. Now I'm hot, skin prickling and itchy. The absolute power, the horrific potential of this decision parts my lips. I am literally panting. I'm not sure what will come out of my mouth, but one way or another, it will affect us all.

"Everyone over there," Logan says to my left.

I jump at the sound of his voice.

His left arm is raised, pointing to the rocky wall to the side. His fist is clenched so hard that his forearm is rigid, flexed like he's lifting. The sun reflects off his watch face like a muzzle flash.

Behind us, the other two stop a step back, but close enough to see what he's pointing at. I have to physically stifle a shudder at the sensation of them so near my back up here. Not that I'm close enough to the edge to be pushed, but the sensation of being up high, beyond tree cover, is uncanny.

None of us move.

Logan's jaw tightens. He scowls at all three of us. "No one is going near the edge. We'll sit by the wall. All of us. Now."

The relief that lifts through me makes me feel too light, like I might float away on the breeze.

He's got some plan. I don't have to choose what's next. The

weight of the outcome won't be all on me. Whether he's got the right idea or not—if there even is a right idea—whatever comes of it won't be my fault.

I'm so grateful that I truly don't hesitate. I start walking over to the rock wall. It's as good an idea as any I've come up with. I've always wanted him to be more decisive, to not always defer to me in some chivalric gesture. This is a good time for him to change.

I'm almost to the wall, the sound of the others following me, when I freeze.

Change?

Allison reaches the wall near me, leans against the rock like she might slide down it to a seat.

Logan has dropped his pointed finger and is following Bryce to come rest beside us.

But my mind is spinning. I look back and forth between them, trying to get my mind to reframe the things that have happened.

These are surreal circumstances. Impossible. I can't really know how Logan would act, can I? Who of us knows what we'd do in a situation we've never been in, much less never imagined?

But I do know. Somehow, my gut knows. Logan and I have been together for fifteen years, since we were teenagers. I know him, good, bad, and grating, and for fifteen years I've wished he would stop defaulting to my decisions. From the big ones, like having kids or not, to the little ones, like what movie to watch or where to eat, he's put me first both when I've been delighted by it and when it's been a burden.

As much as a relief as it was to have someone else decide what's next, that doesn't match up with the Logan I've known.

I don't think the Logan I've been walking beside for this last leg of the hike is my Logan.

It's the other.

CHAPTER 20
LOGAN

I didn't expect Bryce to take control, but it doesn't change my plan. Not really. I've sort of automatically followed the others, moving away from the drop-off and toward the rock wall, but it's now or never.

As Bryce is turning to follow us over, I tackle him.

One of the Elises gasps. The other one shouts, "Hey!"

I plow my shoulder into his lower back, shoving him forward. The only sound that comes from him is a winded ough. He puts his hands out to break his fall, which is what I expected. I let my body follow him down, hands swooping around to knock his out from under him.

His chin cracks the ground as he jerks his head up to avoid smashing his face. I swipe his arms around, yank them behind his back.

I played football in middle school, wrestled in high school. He might look exactly like me, might have the same physical advantage, but he didn't do what I did. He doesn't have the muscle memory of tackling and pinning.

I use my knee and all of my weight to pin him, but even so, I'll only be able to hold him for so long.

"Elise," I yell, too keyed up to adjust my volume. "Help me!"

I suspect the real Elise will. Even if she's not sure I'm me, won't she hear it? Won't she hear me call for her help and do it instinctually?

I glance up.

They're both scrambling to help.

Well, shit.

Kind of. Less clarity, but double help. Okay.

"My watch band," I say between heavy breaths. "Hold him." I look at the Elise on my right and point with my nod at Bryce's arm. "All your weight, right there."

She copies me, pressing both knees into his arm, pinning it to the dirt instead of into his back. He hisses in pain. Good enough.

"You, there," I say to the Elise on my left.

Swallowing, she does. Her hands tremble ever so slightly. Could be real, could be acting.

I keep my knees down, but let go with my hands, undoing my watch band. I fumble for a second, take a deep breath. I've never done anything like this in my life. I take another breath, then carefully unhook the watch face, slipping it into my shirt pocket under my quarter-zip. Then I unknot the end of the braided rope and start tugging it open, each section coming loose and pulling the next with it as it was designed. I end up with about three feet of cordage.

On either side of me, the Elises also breathe heavily. I can smell us, or at least myself. Sweat and fear. The dirt up here, dry but rich.

"Wrists together," I tell the girls, and Bryce only struggles until I put a knee at his balls, ready to press, then he goes still.

Then it's a matter of tying his wrists together. I take his watch off, put it in my pocket, and wrap the paracord from my own around and around, tight, and knot it. I'm not an expert at knots, but I know enough from scouts and rock climbing to do a job that won't be undone right away. Can he eventually find a sharp rock and saw through the cord? Maybe. But not with me watching.

Bryce starts to roll to his side, presumably to get his knees under him and try to stand, but I put my weight on his back again. "No. Stay down."

A little surprisingly, he does.

Both of the Elises, though, scramble away.

It makes my guts sink, to sense she's afraid of me. They're afraid of me. Which one of them is the real Elise?

I look up, back and forth between them, and I realize that in the scuffle, I lost track of which is which. Not that I knew for sure, but I thought I knew. Now I'm not even sure which one is the one I thought was the real Elise.

They both stop several feet away, backed up to the rock wall farthest from the cliff edge. They both have wide eyes, guarded posture, like prey ready to bolt, and damn that's a shitty feeling.

In all our years together, I don't think Elise has ever seen me get physical with someone. I've never had to in front of her. Maybe I've used my size a time or two to make creeps back up, but

I definitely haven't been in a fight since I was a kid. Hopefully she'll understand that it was to keep us safe, but then again, she might not know I'm me. She might think she's staring at Bryce.

She might think she's next.

CHAPTER 21
ELISE

The decisiveness of the lead Logan had all but convinced me I had it wrong, that he's Bryce, until the other Logan jumped him. My first thought was that Logan would never do that, attack somebody, but then I realized he might. In a situation like this, where we're near a precipice, impossibly entangled, with no safety in sight? He might.

In the intensity of the scuffle, I barely hesitated to help him tie the other Logan up. The way he asked for my help was innate, and I responded innately. Even when I began to question it, as he undid his survival bracelet, I stuck with it, because Allison helped too, without question, and I knew if I refused, he'd think I was her.

I know already, just moments after it's been done, that I'll be haunted by this for the rest of my life. If I survive, I'll have nightmares forever. Logan as a victim, assaulted. Logan as an attacker, restraining someone. Logan as a villain, contained. Logan as a hero, taking risks. Right now, as I stare at them both, the man

I married face-down in the dirt and the man I married pinning him there, they all feel true. They all look and seem possible. In my mind, every conceivable variation of Logan has acted itself out, and I'll never be able to forget them.

And me? Yes.

Me and what I've done. I am all of the results of this choice, all at once, right now and forever.

I back away from them both, all, scooting until I feel the solidity of the rock at my back. Allison, to my left. Logan and the other Logan in front of us, one pinning the other. If I helped Bryce tie up Logan instead of the reverse, I'm done for. I'll be outnumbered and at their mercy. I don't even know what they want.

For a moment, my mind goes all the way still. Blank. No thoughts, just waiting.

Waiting for what happens next.

The Logan who's tied up lifts his face off the ground to glance at us, and he spits to get dirt out of his mouth, and I know.

With that one tiny gesture, I know.

Logan—the real Logan, my Logan—spits weird. He always has. It's an unimportant quirk that I rarely think about, even when I see him doing it, because I'm so used to it. I've watched him brush his teeth hundreds, thousands of times. He spits carefully, out of the middle-side of his lips instead of the very center, a slower, more intentional drop of spit than anyone else I've seen. We've joked about it before. We've joked about practically everything about each other that's odd or noteworthy over the years and years of being together. It's fodder for fun, for discussion. I've teased him.

Questioned him. He doesn't know why he spits that way exactly, because he doesn't remember ever spitting the "normal" way. He does raise the effective point that it doesn't splatter as much, so he doesn't make a mess, but he honestly can't remember if that's why he started it as a kid. Why out of the off-center part of his lips instead of the middle? He can never say. A shrug, a baffled laugh. He just does.

But he always does, and not just when he brushes his teeth in front of me. I've seen him when he thought he was alone. I've seen him spit for other reasons too. Getting out cold-weather-exercise phlegm. Bad taste, gross food. Sexy stuff. And never once have I ever seen him spit with force from centered lips.

The Logan who's tied up just did. A totally normal way to spit dirt from his mouth.

Which makes him "Bryce," the other one, the fake.

He knows what Logan knows, but not all at once? Like they can access our memories but not hold them in lived experience. Maybe if he'd stopped to question how Logan would spit, he would've matched it but didn't think to check for something so specific. It's given him away.

I look at Logan, still hovering over him to make sure he doesn't try to get up, and it's Logan. It really is.

I know it with every cell of my being, finally, for sure.

The relief I feel leaves me limp, collapsing into the rock wall at my back like I might pass out. I didn't just help some evil mimic tie up my husband. I chose right, Logan did the right thing, and I know he's really him.

Bryce's eyes are wide, like he's searching for answers, and I think I see when he finds them, within the database of his own mind—or Logan's. His face goes tight, then blank. He's still. I think he's just figured out that I know.

All of a sudden, we're half of the way there. Halfway to together. Halfway to safe.

Now I need to find a way to help Logan see that I'm the real me.

CHAPTER 22
LOGAN

"Okay," I say, looking from one Elise to the other. "Who's who?"

The Elise on the left snorts a laugh. I lock eyes with her. It's Elise's real snort, which I rarely hear unless she's truly caught off guard by something. I raise my eyebrows.

She glances at the other Elise, then scowls, then sort of shrugs. "Well?" The well captures it. I was thinking out loud more than actually asking them, because of course Allison isn't going to just come clean now. Just raise her hand and admit she's the fake because I asked.

The ludicrous urge to laugh rises in me, and I clamp it down. Not just because I need to focus, but because I don't know if the one who snorted is the real one. I guess the other one could know how Elise snorts when she's surprised by a laugh. I don't want to feel solidarity with one of them if I can't be sure it's legit.

I swallow, thinking. They might not realize that I've fully lost track of them. It's not like I was certain I had the right Elise, but I was leaning toward the one who had the tissues. That's a concrete difference. "Empty your pockets," I tell them both.

I'm not sure if they will—the real Elise might not think I'm the real Logan, after all—but they do. The Elise on my right pulls out the packet of travel tissues. The Elise on my left, the one who snorted, has nothing in any of her pockets.

"Okay," I say, indicating the left one with no tissues. I'm glad I didn't share a chuckle with her since she's probably Allison. "Take off your jacket so it's easier to tell you apart."

She doesn't hesitate. She unzips the top and pulls the fleece over her head, maybe even with the relief that comes with removing a layer when you're warm. Her mannerisms are Elise, for sure, but they've both used some, haven't they? I'm afraid that's not enough. I'm searching my mind for some magical-definitive question I can ask them when she interjects, "My jacket!"

All three of us look at her, confused, waiting.

She pushes to standing, still clinging to the rock wall at her back, but clearly elated by something. She holds out her palms, as if their emptiness is proof positive instead of negative. "My tissues are in the pocket of my rain jacket, not my pants! When you asked me earlier, I forgot. After I used one to wipe, I stuck the packet in my jacket pocket instead of my pants like usual because I was still squatting and I didn't want to set them in the dirt. I forgot they were in there. I took off my rain jacket this morning when we were packing up so it wouldn't make noise as we were leaving. They're back at camp!"

Her face is so triumphant, so animated, so goddamn hopeful that I want to believe her. I love when her eyes get big and shiny like this, like she's spotted beauty and wants to share it with me.

I want to believe her so much it makes my chest hurt. I have to swallow the urge to say her name.

"Well, of course you'd say something like that," the other Elise accuses. "You've had all day to make up a reason why you don't have my tissues. But I always carry these on trips, and I always put them in my pants pocket, not my jacket."

"We can go back to camp and see," she challenges.

The Elise on the right throws back, "See what? That you can materialize some now that you realize you were supposed to have them all along? No thanks. That doesn't prove anything."

My hope tastes sour. I almost fell for that. True or not, I almost thought it was proof. I want to know so badly, but I can't let that make me jump to a conclusion too soon. This is too important for me to wishful-think it. This is Elise. This is everything.

To me, the Elise on the right says, "You know I always keep my tissues in the same pocket. I get them out too often to shift them around. I need to be able to grab one when I start sneezing."

That is true. The sneezing is inevitable, especially in the spring when allergies are blooming.

It's pretty convincing, the way the right Elise says it like it's known fact.

It's also pretty convincing, the way the left Elise is watching me with hope and trust and fear in her eyes.

And I no longer have any idea which Elise is the real Elise.

Below me, Bryce has been placid. He turned his face to the side to breathe easier, but he hasn't fought back again. Strange. Is it because he's okay with staying here? Is he content to stay behind as long as it's the other Elise that walks away beside me?

After all, if what they want is to infiltrate us somehow, only one of them needs to make it back. If they both wanted to, I think killing us would've been way easier than this. They could've jumped us overnight and then morphed to look like us. It seems like what they really want is a single replacement, not a double. I consider telling Bryce he can sit up, but I'm not feeling charitable. I do let myself take my knee away from his crotch, though, and squat more comfortably behind him instead.

"Tell me something I don't know yet," I tell them. Elise and Elise. "One at a time. You," I interrupt, before either of them can speak. I point to the Elise on the right, who has the tissues in her hand still, like proof. "Tell me something new."

"New?"

"Yeah. Not something we've already done. Tell me something about right now. Or the future," I blurt, finally having an idea. "Tell me what you think about the reason we came out here to begin with."

It's hard to believe this is actually the same trip we decided to take to reconnect and talk about our future together. We came out here with issues we needed to work out and the sense of a breaking point looming. I half thought we'd work it out and half thought she'd ask for a divorce. It all seems far away now, like a separate trip. Or like this trip is separate, an island of impossibility in an otherwise normal life.

The Elise on the right swallows, tucks the tissue packet with her hand back into her pants pocket. She's sitting. I see her gaze flick down to Bryce's, in front of me, then back to me. "Okay," she drawls in a soft voice. "You want to know if I've made a decision."

It's not quite a question, but I nod. Beneath and in front of me, Bryce is still, silent. So is the Elise on the left. It makes the whole moment seem paused as the Elise on the right thinks.

She shifts to be on her knees, not kneeling but back on her heels. Her hands rest on her legs, arms locked. When her eyes meet mine, my breath catches.

"Yes," she says. "I do."

I don't breathe.

She doesn't go on.

"You do what?" I finally force out.

"I do want to have kids."

There's a cleaving feeling through my chest, from down in my guts. Like a big zipper being pulled. My throat is so tight I don't trust it to speak. I just stare at her. Elise. My Elise.

Her eyes shimmer with tears, like a gleam from within the mild shade of the rock behind her. "Of course I do, babe. I've always wanted us to have babies. It's always been the plan. I just. . ." her gaze circles the sky, the vista, comes back to me. She tries to shrug, but leaning forward on her arms makes it weird. "I just got scared. I got all in my head about it. I'm still scared. But being out here. All this? It's made one thing look so clear to me now. I want kids. With you. We'll never feel complete unless we try. I'm ready now."

It's what I want to hear. It's what I've ached to hear for so long. For years.

The only thing that keeps me from running to her, from swooping her into my arms and hugging her as hard as I can, is Bryce. My doppelganger, this knockoff, so still lying between us.

And then, to the left. I let my eyes land on her. The other Elise.

CHAPTER 23
ELISE

My eyes are so wide, so filled with unshed tears, that I see Logan through a blur of water. I can't look away from his face. I watched it the whole time Allison spoke. I watched his hope, his yearning, his relief. His joy. Blurrier and blurrier, I watched him grasp a possibility of the future he wants. The one we planned for.

The one I don't want anymore.

I know that now. I was beginning to understand it before, but now, hearing someone say in my exact voice the answer he so deeply wants me to give him, I can't deny it. What she said is not what's true. It's not what I want. I've tried to want it, tried to change my own mind back to when we were young, but I can't.

It would be a lie.

"You," he says gruffly, and I can see through the waterfall shimmering between him and my eyes that he means me. "Your turn."

I blink, and the tears spill in fast rolls down my cheeks. I blink a lot to clear my eyes, creating my own waterfall. I wish I could go back in time, to when we stood shivering in the skinny dipping pool holding on to each other. We thought that everything was wrong and breaking, but we had each other. We had all we needed.

And now everything really is breaking.

I don't want to say it.

I don't want to hurt him, to crush him. I don't want to make him resent me, or regret marrying me. I don't want to tear us apart.

But now there's even more, because he doesn't know I'm me, I don't think. I've figured out he's him, but he's obviously still trying to tell if I'm me or Allison. And if I tell him no, I don't want kids after all, will he believe I'm me? Or will his hope cloud his judgement?

Or worse, a dark thought occurs to me. Will he simply prefer her? Choose her?

He said he loves me. Me for me. He said he can be happy without kids, but he can't be happy without me. Does that hold true if he can have a facsimile instead? A me who's almost me, only better?

I still stand against the rock wall behind me, from when I stood earlier to dig through my pockets. I'm glad I do, because my body has started shaking. Literally shaking like I'm about to pass out. I press my back into the rock, grab the rough surface with both hands, try to breathe.

See me, I think at him, staring across the plateau into his eyes. My chest is rising and falling fast, and tears are still falling, collecting beneath my chin. See me, know me, want me.

I could lie, of course, but then I'd hate myself for the rest of my life. I'd either be committing to a future I now know isn't the one for me, or I'd be tricking him. I don't want to trick him.

With a deep breath that sounds more like a gasp, I say it: "I don't."

His face barely changes, but I see it. I see the way he holds it from falling.

"I don't," I say again, dropping my gaze from his. I can't watch the micro expressions sink his features. "I tried, but I just don't." My voice climbs higher and higher as my throat constricts around crying. The last words are squeezed out in squeaks that might be funny in other circumstances. "Not anymore. I'm sorry." I lean forward, dropping my head and sinking to a seat as sobs take hold.

They're big sobs, the kind that come rarely. If I were home, I'd collapse on the bed and let them go. Here, I hug my knees to my chest and try to breathe.

I'm trying to figure out what to do, how to handle whatever is next, but all I can think is that Logan will leave me. My heart is breaking.

Movement snaps my head up. Logan is almost to me. I gasp, hope nearly lifting me to my feet to meet him. The urge to tackle hug him.

Then my gaze drops, and I notice what's in his hands. The rope. The long, strong cording from his survival band—no, from Bryce's watch band this time—like he used to tie up Bryce. He's unwound it already, and he's got it stretched out across both palms.

"No," I say, shoving back, but my back is already against the wall. I can't get farther.

He squats in front of me. "Put your hands out. In fists, wrists together."

"No," I say again, and then he winks at me.

"Don't make this ugly," he says, talking over any reaction I might have. "Just do it. Elise," he says, glancing at Allison. "Come help me tie her."

He looks down at my hands, which I lift like I'm in a dream and my body isn't actually under my control. I try to meet his eyes again. He did wink, right? I didn't make that up. It was so fast. Not exaggerated. No other facial motion with it. Just the left eye, the side away from Allison.

It could be a trick.

He could have winked to make me pliable, to believe he thinks I'm me and he has some plan. If I keep my wrists out, they might just tie me up and leave together. Leave me here alone.

No, not alone. Worse than alone.

My gaze lifts around Logan to see Bryce, who still lies in the dirt, watching everything with silent, appraising eyes. Eyes that look like my husband's but are definitely not my husband's. It's like, now that he knows his disguise is blown, he's stopped trying to inhabit Logan's personality, his essence. It's like he's let the Logan drain out of him.

The rope touches my skin, and I jerk my eyes back to the real Logan's. He meets them for a second, a moment, then back down to the rope as Allison makes her way over. She puts a hand on his shoulder, sinks to kneel beside him. "What do you want me to do?" she asks in my voice.

"Just hold her arm," he says.

I consider hitting her. A tackle, maybe? A punch? I don't know how to fight, but if Logan's wink was just sweat in his eye—or a trap—I can't just keep my hands out and let them tie me up, can I?

Her hands are both on my forearm, which puts her wrists close to mine. I'm one twitch from jumping on her when he shifts the rope. Four inches right, and it's under hers.

He wraps it upward. Her eyes widen. I jerk my arms down to get her hands off me, then grab her arms as fast as I can. "No!" she gasps.

I have her by the elbows. I bend my own elbows wide as far as I can so Logan can get through with the cord. She tries to bend hers, and I squeeze them as hard as I can to keep them straight.

"Behind her back," he says, and we switch around so her wrists are behind her.

It's awkward, fumbling, but we do it. Logan wraps her wrists like Bryce's. He's knotting it when I hear something.

"Ah!" I shout, no word to the sound, just panic.

Bryce is shoving to his feet, hands behind his back.

"Stop," Logan yells, loud and firm.

Surprisingly, Bryce kind of does. He doesn't have momentum, or even the element of surprise. He takes a step toward us, testing, and Logan says, "Your arms are tied up. Do you really want to test a shoving match up here?"

All four of us look to the drop off several yards away.

Bryce straightens his posture, making it clear he's not going to charge for a tackle.

Logan jerks his head to the side toward the trail, farther down the rock wall. "Sit down over there. Keep going. There. Sit." He's tying the cord while he instructs and watches. Once it's secure, he starts shifting Allison to sit back against the wall.

She twists to put her hand on his as he moves her. "This is wrong," she tells him, trying to meet his gaze. "You've got it wrong, babe. I'm not mad. Okay? I'm scared. I'm really scared. You have me wrong. Please, untie me. Please. We can figure this out."

CHAPTER 24
LOGAN

It's a mindfuck how real she looks. Staring at me from inches away, soft hand on my hand, voice just exactly Elise's voice.

"Sit here," I say calmly, and I can tell she's confused how to interpret it.

Any doubt I had that I was wrong went away when Bryce stood up. The whole time I was trying to tell who's who, he was content to watch. The whole time Allison gave her "let's have babies together" speech, he was still. Even when Elise talked, he was silent. But when I moved to tie up Allison, he got up.

Because one of them wants to go home with us. Not both. He was okay with staying behind as long as Allison was the one to head back with me, but if they've both been figured out, he needed to make a move.

So yeah, Elise is Elise, and I got it right.

Elise tackles me.

A fleeting thought that I am wrong, that she's Allison. She catches me just right to knock some wind out of me, but I grab her, squeeze her back. She hugs me as hard as she can. I lift her off her feet. She's mumbling something directly into my jacket. "What?" I say, leaning down to feel her hair tickle my jaw even as I keep an eye on the other two.

"I'm me," she says. She's saying it over and over. "I'm me. I'm me. I'm me." It's part relief, part fear, part plea.

"I know," I assure her. "I know. And I'm me."

She pulls back in my arms enough to look up at my face. Then she spares a glance over her shoulder to check the others as well. They both watch us intently but haven't tried to move. "How'd you know?" she asks me quietly, reaching to touch the sides of my face like confirmation.

"Your answer," I say. "About not wanting kids." I hate that my voice cracks a bit when I say it, but there it is.

"You knew that would be my answer?"

"No. Maybe? Maybe. But no, I knew because you gave it, even though it was hard and you didn't want to say it and it obviously would've been easier and more. . ." I wave a hand at the lack of word choices that come to me, "whatever to say what you thought I wanted to hear. But you didn't. You told me the truth, even during all of this. That's so freaking brave, Elise. I don't know anyone else with that kind of integrity. It had to be you."

Her eyes are full of tears again, but this time she's smiling up at me. I think for a second she might kiss me, but she looks over her shoulder again.

"How did you know I'm me?" I ask, also checking the others again. We instinctively keep our voices low.

Her smile morphs from emotional to mischievous. "He spits normal," she says.

"Huh?"

"When he spits. He doesn't spit like a weirdo," she says, miming the controlled way I spit from the side of my mouth.

The laugh that hoots out of me is so loud it echoes for a second, rebounding off the rock wall behind us and carrying out through the vista like an animal's cry of freedom.

CHAPTER 25
ELISE

There aren't other places to talk up here that afford more privacy. The space is open, with no trees or bushes, no rails, nothing to step behind. Besides, the longer we stand up here with them, the eerier it feels. It's a terrible place to have any sort of physical altercation. We're lucky they don't seem to want us hurt or killed.

"Should we tie their ankles too?" Logan murmurs. "So they can't follow us?"

"With what?"

"We could split my watch cord, but we'd have to untie them to do it. Maybe use our jacket sleeves?"

I swallow, looking at the two of them, just like the two of us. Maybe we should kill them. We could push them off the cliff, make sure they're all the way gone, but there's just the tiniest sliver of a doubt. It's a shadow, but a shadow of a possibility of killing my partner is too much. No, I don't want to kill them. "Let's do that," I agree.

We use our own sweaters, because their hands tied together

make theirs too hard to get off. Bryce seems to be content to let us tie his feet together, but Allison cries and asks Logan to stop the whole time. It's brutal.

We stand, and as soon as I slide my hand down Logan's arm to take his hand, Allison says, "Where are you going?" Panic lines her voice. "Logan? Where are you going?"

As we head toward the trailhead, Logan looks over his shoulder at her. "We're just going to go talk. We're not leaving."

His willingness to answer her, and maybe even comfort her, gives me pause. Is he just trying to get her not to make trouble, or is he actually doubting me?

He gives my hand a squeeze, but he doesn't look me in the eyes.

Are we going to wonder forever?

"Please," she begs. "Please, don't go. Don't walk away. Logan. Allison. Please. Please."

Her desperate, terrified tone almost has me feeling sorry for her until she says her own name to me. Hearing it severs the heartstrings she's tugged on.

"Logan," she sobs. "Please don't leave me here with him!"

I clasp Logan's hand even tighter and pull him with me.

CHAPTER 26
LOGAN

The relief of finally holding Elise's hand doesn't last long, not with the other Elise—Allison, I correct myself—crying behind us as we walk back toward the trail. No matter how sure I feel that Elise is really Elise, hearing her voice begging me not to walk away is unnerving. Bryce is silent, which is almost as discomforting, but I just want her to be quiet so I can think.

"We'll be right back!" I practically shout back at her. When Elise looks at me, I feel guilty.

We go a little bit down the trail—just far enough that they can't see us, but we can step around a bend to check that they're still sitting where we left them. We can still hear Allison yelling, but they definitely won't be able to hear us talking in hushed voices.

As soon as we have this sliver of privacy, Elise whispers, "What are we going to do?"

I make myself look her in the eyes. I sigh. It's her. It's still her. For sure.

But didn't I think that already when I was wrong?

I shake my head at my thoughts, then again at her question. "I don't know."

She drops my hand so she can wring hers together. I can see her mind working. She's thinking I won't decide this. She's thinking it's up to her. She shakes her hands out, like she's twisted them too hard.

"Maybe," I start, and her eyebrows shoot up, hopeful. Allison has stopped screaming, probably to try to hear us. I drop my low voice to a full whisper. "Maybe we. . . push them? Over the edge?"

"Kill them?"

As soon as she says it, I want to snatch the idea back. I hate to admit it, but I'm not one hundred percent sure I can't be wrong about Elise. Ninety-nine point nine-nine-nine is not one hundred. What if that fraction of a decimal is the love of my life? I have a brief imagining of us old, and after decades more of being together, somehow realizing I'd gotten it wrong, that it had been Allison with me the whole time. If I am wrong, I can't risk being end-her-life wrong. I just can't.

"I don't know. I don't know," I mutter. "We don't know what they are, why they're doing this. What else can we do?"

"Just leave them here."

I glance back, step to the side to make sure they're still there. They are. To Elise, I ask, "Tied up?"

She nods. "I mean, we can't untie them and then walk away. I don't want to risk getting mixed up again. Will they be able to untie themselves?"

I swallow, mentally reviewing my knots. "I don't think so. Their wrists are behind their backs, so they won't be able to see what they're doing to help each other. They can probably saw through the paracord eventually, if they find a sharp rock?"

"Do you have the pocketknife in your pocket?"

I shake my head, wondering if she wants to cut them free, but then I realize if I have one, he might have one, like the tissues. "No, it's in my backpack." I wait, thinking. "If they're able to get loose, it'll take a while. We'll have a really good head start."

She swallows, hugs her elbows. She used her fleece jacket to tie Allison's ankles. I want to put my hands out, rub her arms to warm her in this shade, but I'm afraid she doesn't trust me any more. I'm afraid we might never be able to trust each other all the way ever again.

Fuck that. I put my hands on her arms. She doesn't quite flinch, but she goes still. I wait for her to shrug me off, step back, or tell me to stop. She doesn't, so I do the friction warming thing, draw her into me.

"I hate this," I tell her.

She melts into me, nods.

"Do you have a different idea?"

We're silent for a moment, and Allison calls, "Logan?"

We both look toward the voice, but don't move.

"They'll be okay for a while," I point out. "Days, even if they can't get untied. Eventually someone else will probably hike this trail and find them."

"I don't know if that's better or worse," Elise murmurs, pulling out of my arms.

"Me either," I admit. If they do eventually get free, where will they go? Will they try to come find us? Or will they approach some other couple on the trail, slowly changing to look like them? "But I do think it's better than untying them or pushing them over the edge."

She nods, slowly into quickly, like she's talking herself through it. "Yeah, okay," she finally says. "We'll leave them. Should we. . ." She trails off, because what else is there? Go tell them goodbye?

"Let's just go," I whisper. "No reason to delay."

"Logan?" Allison calls again, her crying sounding panicked now, like she can sense we're going to leave.

I can feel my pulse so hard in my throat, my Adam's apple vibrates with it. I swallow, and it feels too high up. I gesture in front of me, a hiking habit to let her set the pace.

She hesitates a second, and I'm not sure if it's because of leaving them or because of turning her back to me. Then she moves, quietly, down the trail. I follow.

I think we're pretty quiet, but after a few yards Allison starts really screaming. Fully panicked, raw terror. It's so convincing.

Elise and I start running.

CHAPTER 27
ELISE

This trail isn't good for running. Too many roots. I've stumbled twice, almost twisted my ankle. Eventually our pace slows to a jog. Then about ten, fifteen minutes after that, we stop.

Our panting breaths are the only sound for a while. When those calm, I hear the hollow patter of a woodpecker, the grating creak of insects. Eventually, leaves in the wind. I don't hear the other couple following us. No footsteps. No more yelling.

Logan stretches his arms behind his head. "Do you want to walk now?"

I nod, pulse slowing, fatigued. A wild swirl of emotions. Fear. Guilt. Victory. Doubt. Relief.

"They stopped yelling sooner than I thought they would."

"I guess they've given up."

Neither of us says anything. I never would've given up yelling if Logan had gotten it wrong, left me behind with Bryce. It makes me feel more secure that we chose correctly, but it also makes me wonder what they'll do now. Will they wait around up there for someone else to come by and untie them? Will they try again until someone takes them home?

Why?

Logan lets me take the lead, as usual, and we walk at a calmer pace back down the trail—looking over our shoulders more than usual. After a long time of walking, maybe half an hour or more, my thoughts have slowed enough to start rummaging through the past and future. Are we ever going to feel safe again? What the hell was that? Did we do the right thing? What will we do now?

"Are you—" I start, then cut myself off. Absurd how we've just gone through all of this and it's still hard to talk about my damn feelings. I swallow, shake my head at myself. "Is what you said still true? About being happy with just me?"

There's a smile in his tone. "You think I changed my mind between the vista and here?"

I send him a relieved smirk, because he wouldn't be teasing me if the answer had actually changed. "No, but maybe after hearing me actually say it out loud for the first time?"

"No. Still just need you, Elise. Forever includes all of the options, even if they're not the original ones."

We're not that far from camp, I think. I press, "You don't think you're going to resent me? Over time?"

"I don't think so," he says. "I never have before. And I guess if I do then we'll have to figure it out, right? That doesn't change anything for me."

It's such an honest answer, not denying the possibility of it creeping in, that it actually does soften my worry.

We break through the trees on a downhill stretch of trail, and I finally see our campsite. The others' tent is still pitched, ours collapsed where we left it when they interrupted us this morning, the backpacks stacked nearby.

Between the tents and the campfire, on the ground, there's a little blue oval with a canopy over part of it, about the size of a small desktop or a large suitcase. "What is that?" I murmur.

"Hm?" Logan asks, peering past me.

We walk closer, and I stare at it, trying to tell what it is. It wasn't there before. It definitely wasn't there when we left camp with the other couple this morning. It's a bright, vivid shade of baby blue. It looks inflatable, down low on the grass, and as I stare, something inside it moves.

CHAPTER 28
LOGAN

Elise gasps, "Oh my God. That's a baby," and rushes into camp.

My mouth hangs open, and I follow. She's right. At first, I couldn't tell what the blue thing was, but it's a little nylon bassinet crib-type thing. It has a little partial cover, and inside, nestled in white padding, is a baby.

"What the hell?" I ask the air. Elise makes a beeline toward the baby, but I'm scanning the area. Maybe someone came to this campsite while we were up at the vista? But I don't see anyone, don't see any gear but ours and the other couple's. "Did they have a baby with them?" I ask incredulously. "Could they have had a baby the whole time and we didn't notice?"

I remember seeing Bryce carrying something when they first hiked into camp at the same time as us and thinking it looked like a baby in one of those chest carriers people use, but it had definitely not been a baby. He'd drawn his backpack around to the front to get something out of it, and there was no way they could've had an infant with them and us not have seen it.

Not to mention camping all night? Even if it was the quietest baby in the world, it would've made some sounds at some point, and they would've had to feed it and stuff. No, this baby wasn't with them, and it wasn't here when we left camp either. No one is nearby. The camp is empty except for us.

"We have to call someone," Elise says over her shoulder as she rushes to check on the baby. "Either its parents got hurt or lost or—or they abandoned it. Grab your phone!" As she nears, she slows, looking at the little thing as it lifts two tiny fists in the air with footied feet. "Did someone leave you here?" she coos as she edges closer, speaking in that universal baby tone.

I can't help continuing to scan for adults nearby, for a backpack, a water bottle. Something. But the only things I see are ours and the other's. I dig my dry bag out of my backpack and pull out my phone.

The screen blinks on, my lockscreen photo shuffle on an old, old picture of Elise and me on that college tour trip around Europe. In fact, we're standing in front of the cathedral I'd just mentioned yesterday that looked like it was dripping. She said Porto, but I knew it was Madrid. As I swipe the screen open, I notice a sign in the background that says Barcelona. Barcelona?

Neither of us was right. I shake my head, finishing the swipe. Crazy how two different people could remember something we both experienced completely wrong.

I open my phone app to dial. . . what? 911, I guess. But there's no signal out here. Of course. "We won't be able to call anyone until we get back to the trailhead." I tuck it into my pocket.

I turn to see Elise standing at the bassinet now, bending over it to pick up the infant. I have a moment of cringing, like someone will catch her picking up their child and be outraged at the uninvited contact, but the feeling slips away on surprise as I see how naturally she scoops it up. She doesn't pick it up the way I might've—hesitant, delicate, unfamiliar. She picks it up as if she's picked it up a thousand times before, raising it easily into her arms and even lifting it up to smile at it. Its fat little arms smush comfortably between its body and her chest as she plants an easy kiss on the top of its hat.

The surprise I feel at the gesture is so unexpected that I stall, frozen in my movement toward them.

She stands at the blue bassinet in its patch of bright green grass, and I stand halted a few yards away. I'm close enough to see the baby's eyes. It wears a soft blue beanie on its tiny head. It looks at me over my wife's shoulder with the vivid blue eyes some newborns keep for a while, but so intelligent for a moment that I feel a strange electric current sizzle up my sweaty neck.

"Well, let's pack up and get going?" she prompts, as if I've been standing around for an hour. "I can't wait to get home."

The first attempt at a response isn't a word at all. It's a choking sound. I clear my throat, step toward them. "Elise," I squeeze out. It's so squeaky I clear it an extra time. "Elise." Is she having some kind of breakdown? An acute post-traumatic stress response? "Sweetie," I urge, softening my shock at her bizarre calm about this abandoned kid by making my voice extra gentle. "We don't know whose baby that is."

She rolls her eyes with a half-smile, like I'm clearly joking. To the baby, she says, "Daddy is so silly." To me, still looking at him, she says affectionately, "We've always known him. He's always been here."

I am static with wrongness. I move toward her, stepping from brown leaves to green grass.

She turns to smile at me, and the happiness on her face makes me catch my breath.

I step into her side, wrap my arms around them both. I inhale his sweet, familiar baby scent, plant a kiss on his round little cheek. "How about you, buddy? You ready to start hiking again?"

He coos at me, kicking.

Elise smiles. "Harrison is ready. Aren't you, bubba? Yes, you are."

Watching the way he gives her his big toothless smile, it's hard to imagine any other outcome than this one. It's almost impossible to believe that we were just contemplating divorce—of becoming a split-parent home when he's not even one year old.

Elise looks at me, almost seeming to read my mind, and gives me that look. That knowing, couple look that means everything at once. "I think the chest carrier is still in the backpack," she says.

I nod, moving to dig it out and put it on.

Lots of couples go through a rough patch in their marriage when they add a baby. It shifts everything around, exposes weak spots, adds new complications. But Elise and I are solid. We love each other and Harrison too much not to repair things. I'm glad the three of us came out here to work through it.

She brings him over to slide him into the chest rig, and he gives that foot kick I love when he sees my face.

"Hey, little dude," I say. "You ready for some more hiking?"

I can't wait for us to be back home. The risk of losing each other has made it so clear that being apart is unacceptable. We were slowly crashing, but now we're clear again. Resolved.

Together we get Harrison's little feet through the leg holes and slide him in, the warm weight of him adding to my load welcome despite my fatigue. These small acts of fatherhood still feel fresh, like the first time I ever held him to my chest. I buckle him in and tighten the straps, inhaling that "brand new" smell.

Before I can even ask, Elise is digging out granola bars and handing me one. She rips open a baby bar too and breaks off a bite so he can't throw the whole thing in the dirt.

Actually, it's grass. I step back enough to see that it's a small round circle of that bright green grass, similar to those two overlapping circles earlier, down trail. This one is smaller, only about three feet across, about centered around where we'd set up his inflatable crib. I guess these just pop up around here. It is spring.

We do the load-up routine of getting the tent stuffed away, our packs sorted, the whole deal. There's actually another tent across the fire pit, but no one else is around. I guess someone else pitched it and plans to come back.

When Elise puts her rain jacket into her backpack, she pulls out a packet of tissues and holds it up to me, face confused for a moment. Then she tucks it into her pants pocket, tilts her head, and asks, "Did we take Harrison up to the vista?"

I absently rub his soft cheek with my thumb. For a moment, I can't remember our morning. Then it comes back to me, and I smile. "Of course. Don't you remember the view?"

She squints at me, smiling. "I'm just tired. Let's go home."

It's less than ten minutes before we're ready to go. We hit the trail at a hustle, knowing we won't want to stop until we absolutely have to.

Where the trail is wide enough, we hold hands. Harrison babbles in his nonsense language, and the afternoon grows sunnier still.

We're going to make it, she and I. Our little family. Together, the three of us start the hike back home.

ACKNOWLEDGMENTS

Thank you to Alan Lastufka for planting the seed of a "sequel" to *The Extra* that eventually sprouted and grew into *The Other* and *The Spare*. I might never have started dreaming of what a follow-up could look like if you hadn't mentioned it. Also, thank you for another awesome cover. Campingfolk 4life. You are a true creative partner, and I'm so happy I get to continue working with you.

Thanks to my agent Alec Shane for matching me up with Shortwave and handling the deals so I can keep putting out books. Your work behind the scenes is cheerfully relentless.

Thank you to Kyle, Alex Langley, Kelsey B. Toney, and Dan Hammond Jr. for being my steadfast first readers and support system. Kyle, I can't imagine doing this without you. You're my hero. Kelsey, your willingness to problem-solve and brainstorm until the issues are fixed is unmatched. Dan, your enthusiasm and patience—so many reads!—is so special and valuable to me. Alex, you are such a source of encouragement, ideas, and light. Some days I'm Annie; other days I'm Kyle, Dan, Alex, and Kelsey in a trench coat.

Thanks also to my next rounds of readers: my mom, Molly Jessup, and Lisa Bubert. Every read brought invaluable information that made the book better (and me more calm about a sophomore novella). Thank you also to Nancy LaFever for helping polish away my errors. Thank you to Patricia Santomasso and Sean Patrick Hopkins for helping bring The Outsiders Sequence to life in audio; y'all are a dream team.

Thanks and I'm sorry to all of the people and memories who I gleefully steal tidbits of reality from. Please know that I never lift a person wholesale—only magpie finds. If you ever see a sliver of yourself in any of my stories, it's never used as nonfiction, and it means you live in my mind. And to Kyle, thank you for caring about me and my writing more than what other people might think they know about us because of it.

I also want to thank all of the readers and book people who helped spread the word about *The Extra*. (Shoutout to my mom for being my behind-the-scenes sales person at every bookstore she visits and then some.) Every pre-order, editorial review, Instagram post, podcast mention, Goodreads rating, bookstore suggestion, Facebook comment, shelf display, library request, and excited text to a friend makes a difference. Independent publishing is a labor of love, and the folks out there sharing books they enjoy can literally change the fate of those books.

So thank you, also, to everyone who recommends *The Other* to an unsuspecting friend. If a duplicate copy shows up, then all the better.

ABOUT THE AUTHOR

Annie Neugebauer is a novelist, blogger, nationally award-winning poet, and two-time Bram Stoker Award®-nominated short story author. She writes horror, literary fiction, thriller, science fiction, fantasy, weird fiction, poetry, and anything sharp, dark, and beautiful that might linger in the mind. She has a penchant for high concept ideas and making readers question her mental health.

She's the author of The Outsiders Sequence (*The Extra*, *The Other*, and *The Spare*) and *You Have to Let Them Bleed.*

Visit her at annieneugebauer.com, in most places under @AnnieNeugebauer, or frolicking through the abyss.

A SPECIAL PREVIEW OF

THE SPARE

THE OUTSIDERS SEQUENCE, #3

COMING FROM SHORTWAVE PUBLISHING
MARCH 2027

RULE #1: COME AS YOU ARE

I'm used to being the only one out of the dozen or so of us who doesn't fit in, but this is ridiculous. Every single family member except me is wearing a bright orange hoodie that says *The Schultz Crew* in white letters.

At least now, my brother Dylan's obnoxious sweatshirt makes sense. As he was driving, I couldn't see the lettering on the back, so I thought he'd just developed a penchant for a particularly safety-hazard shade of tangerine, but as we park, I realize everyone else is wearing the same thing.

I swear, if things don't change, this is the last family trip I'm ever going on.

Dylan cuts the engine. I ask, "How do *you* have a hoodie?"

"Mom ordered mine."

"Why didn't she order me one?"

He shrugs. "She said you were in the email chain." He hops out and descends into the fray of orange hugs beneath an RV awning draped in twinkle lights. I let out one unnecessarily audible sigh before opening the passenger side door, just to get it out of my system. One of Meemaw's family rules is *No Whining*, and that includes sighing and eyerolling.

I shut the door, then wipe my dusty hand on my pants. I'm glad I let Dylan bring me. His gray car is coated in thick, rust-orange dirt from the drive. The umber shade is underfoot as far as I can see. It stripes the canyons in the distance—farther, I suspect, than they look—and lines the paths and scrub brush along them.

I've never been out here before, but I looked at pictures of this area online before we came, and I know what I'm seeing is different than peak tourist season. In the spring, summer, and fall, Southerners flock here to hike, camp, and sightsee the second-largest canyon system in the country—mostly in the more popular Palo Duro Canyon State Park, but still in our campground's general area. By now, in early December, Texans have noped right out of here. I haven't seen a single car, camper, or person on our way in. All of the greenery has died back, except for the evergreen Juniper and the prickly pear cacti dotting the orange. The skeletons of deciduous trees and shrubs look strikingly white against all the auburn rock, still as paintings.

Norma shuffles up the slope to meet me at the car. Her hoodie looks bizarre, because she's put it over a long, flowing skirt that's utterly out of place out here in the wilderness. I hope she has leggings on under it, because the Panhandle is supposed to get pretty cold this time of year, especially at night. Not the ideal time for camping, but "Thanksgistmas" must by logic be between Thanksgiving and Christmas, and the canyons were the most central affordable option for everyone to come together this year.

"Come 'ere, snickerdoodle. Give me a squeezerooni."

I smile at her, moving quickly so she doesn't have to make it all the way to me. Norma is a thick, stocky woman who waddles when she walks, and I've never known for sure if she's trying to keep her thighs from chafing or if there's something else going on. Despite the name, Norma is the least normal person in the Schultz family crew, and I love her for it. I wrap her in a hug. The top of her knit hat smells like cinnamon mints and Bengay.

"Hey, Aunt Norma. How's it going?"

"Didn't get the sweatshirt memo?" she asks, leaning away from me without letting go to frown at my dark green sweater and black raincoat.

Before I can ask if there was a literal memo, Jett slams into us and forces his way between me and his mom. "Collision!" he yells, running away.

Norma gives a fake laugh. "He's wired. So excited."

"Oh, I bet," I say, watching him run through the group like a pinball. "How old is he now? Seven?"

"He's *nine*," Norma corrects, eyeing me.

"Wow, nine. Big." She could've said anything between five and thirteen and I would've believed her. All I know is his sweatshirt was ordered in kid sizing.

She smirks like she's seen right through me, but doesn't hold it against me. She links her arm through mine, pulling me down and along as she totters toward the rest of the group.

We've parked on a flat patch slightly above our campsite. The land out here is desolate and grand, with wide, flat swaths of dry dirt and scrubby bare brush topped with dramatic striated ridges and rises. The afternoon sky is overwhelmingly rich blue, dotted with only a few white clouds that look like fakes, the broad expanse of it giving the canyon a run for its money in sheer scope.

The Schultz family reunion site sits in a rusty tea saucer of land consisting of an unlit campfire ring surrounded by folding chairs and log seats beside a picnic table and a charcoal grill canted so far over on its post I'd hesitate to use it. Meemaw's massive RV crowns it all, set up with an awning, lights, chairs, camp table, and décor. A second, smaller RV, my parents' SUV, and their large old-school tan tent spread out around it. We're not, by and large, a serious camping family—think once-a-year RV to supplement a rental house—but we've dispersed enough around Texas and the south now that this year, camping-camping is the setup.

"Look who I've found," Norma sings.

My mom and dad look up at us, but the others must be inside the campers. Mom smiles at me, her smile wilting slightly when she sees that I'm not in the sweatshirt. Dad smirks, then smiles, shaking his head. By the time Norma and I make it down the slope, Mom has rallied. She hugs me. "Hi, sweetie. Meemaw's inside, but you better start setting up your tent. It gets dark quick out here."

I look up at the bright blue sky, but resist commenting. Norma unhooks her arm from mine as if to avoid responsibility. "Wouldn't catch me pitching a tent in this cold," she says, and my brother, already breezing past me to the car to get his gear, calls back, "I don't think we'd catch you pitching a tent anywhere, Aunt Norma."

"Dylan," Mom chastises, as if he's not a grown man. Or what passes for it, at twenty-seven.

But Norma just mutters, "Ain't that the truth."

I turn to go right back where we came from too, but the door to the RV opens. Aunt Feather stands centered in the doorway, balancing a tray of food. Behind her, the pear-shaped shadow of Uncle Glen looms, holding open the door for her.

"Kids," she says, "you made it."

I wonder if there's a cutoff when we'll stop being "kids." When the oldest generation, Meemaw and her brother Beau, die? Because the newest—my nephew Wyatt—is already here, and Dylan, Katie, and I have all finished school and moved out of our parents' house. I'm twenty-four. Perhaps there's some other metric of adulthood that we've yet to hit. Marriage? Homeownership? Katie even has a baby now.

"Hi, Aunt Feather," I say, as she begins to pick her way painstakingly down the collapsible RV steps. She holds herself with a rigid composure that resists her limp from a bad hip. I've always thought she was the least like a feather I can imagine, and that Meemaw must've gotten her and Aunt Norma's names switched. (Mom is Colleen, the balanced middle ground of the older two.)

I move to take the tray from Aunt Feather, but she tsks me away, flicking a disappointed gaze at my outfit. "You never read my emails, Kasper Schultz."

"The sweatshirts?" I ask. I have literally no memory of the email in question, but at least a hundred of them have come through my inbox since the planning of this "vacation" almost a year ago, covering every facet of planning and detail that I had no say in anyway, so somewhere along the line I stopped reading them. Once early on I dared to point out that Austin would've been a few hours longer drive for me than most of them. My aunt got defensive, saying with us spread out how we are now it was hard to pick anywhere truly neutral, and my mom called me and asked me to please not stir the pot.

"Honestly, Kass," Mom says. "I even reminded you."

"Sorry," I mutter to Mom. That I don't have an excuse for. I was probably multitasking.

Aunt Feather begins unloading the contents of her tray onto the camp table centered beneath the string lights. At the close end, a small tabletop Christmas tree wrapped in oversized garland looms over a plastic platter in the shape of a turkey. Propped on the other end of the table is our large wooden *Schultz Family Rules* sign, a decorative monstrosity that lists all of Meemaw's credos like the world's longest *live, laugh, love* poster, which her late husband, my Pop-pop, cut out for her to paint onto. Over Aunt Feather's stiff neck, I see the first line: *Come As You Are*.

Without noticing the irony, Aunt Feather says, "Honestly, I wouldn't mind it except for the photos. She'll stand out like a sore thumb without one. I knew I should've ordered them all, but I wanted Katie to be able to get what size she needed after the baby. I didn't want to have to ask her. New moms are sensitive to that sort of thing."

I don't think my sister Katie much cares about her sizing, given that she's the same size now as before she had Wyatt less than a year ago, but I just repeat my apologies and flee to Dylan's car to get my borrowed tent.

I tell myself I'm picking my battles, but already I feel pressed against reluctance to speak up. I've been telling myself this trip will be different. I won't cave against the impression of making myself a burden. I'll stand up for myself, change the dynamic of how my family treats me. That or try enough to justify skipping these things.

"Hey, Dill," I say, shielded from the campsite by my brother's open trunk. "I'll give you fifty bucks for your hoodie."

To my surprise, he wraps me in a hug, which he hasn't given me yet on this trip. He was already buckled when I got in his car, headed north about two and a half hours from Lubbock where he picked me up on his way from Abilene. My brother is huge, six foot five and muscled like the gym is his job, and the warmth of his hug is so unexpected, so nice, that I just sink into it, feeling for a second like I'm a kid again, but in the good way. The way where no one expects much from you yet and everyone accepts that you belong, and, somehow, because you literally have to be here, you do. I sigh, squeezing him back, and he drops what I think is a kiss on the top of my beanie before yanking his tent bag out of the trunk and striding down the sloped desert path.

Over his shoulder he replies cheerfully, "Not a chance, Kass."

RULE #2: NO SCREENS

The tent I brought is a blue two-person dome shape that I borrowed from my work buddy Tye. He warned me that it's not a winter tent, but I don't have a few hundred dollars sitting around for a one-time trip. Hell, my financial straits are part of why we're out here roughing it instead of cozied up in some made-for-TV cabin rental. I'm too old to still be umbrellaed under my parents' buck, too young to be financially secure yet.

Most of the other Schultz family reunions have been either inside buildings during one holiday or another, or over the summer, like sane people. As a kid, we used to do Thanksgiving, Christmas, and a summer trip. When the aunts started having kids too, we switched to one or the other and sometimes a summer trip. When my siblings and I got old enough to move out of the DFW area, we narrowed it to one. And this year we're between winter holidays because of Katie and Greg having Wyatt; we missed the warm trip and are "making new traditions" or something. I did have to buy a serious sleeping bag, because although it's nice in the sun right now, it might drop below freezing overnight.

Dylan sets up a red triangular tent in half the time it takes me to get mine situated. The earth here is rocky, and I don't have nearly as much weight on me to get the stakes down as he does.

The door to the big RV smacks open and closed, and Katie's voice comes from behind me. "Maybe try hammering instead of pushing," she suggests. My sister never greets me. Our entire lives it's been like one long, sporadic, ongoing conversation.

I glance over my shoulder to see her standing with a hooded bundle that must be Wyatt, my nephew, wrapped in her arms. "Got a hammer?" I ask, struggling to hold the tent's cord taut as I angle the metal stake, but she doesn't laugh.

Instead, she toes a rock toward me. I frown, reaching for it.

Katie is gorgeous as ever, long blonde hair blowing behind her like she's chosen the angle of the wind to flatter her. Our mom is curvy, and our dad is tall. Dylan got the height, Katie got both, and I got neither. She's always looked the way most girls want to look, which is why (I tell myself) our little cousin Charlotte prefers her so much.

On cue, Charlotte slams open the RV door and hops over the steps to land on the ground. The rust orange dirt clouds around her fuzzy winter boots. She's fifteen, built thick like her dad, my Uncle Glen. Her neon orange hoodie is a couple sizes too big for her, and she has both hands shoved so far into the kangaroo pouch that she looks like she has no shoulders.

"Hey Charlotte," I say.

"Hi."

Well, that's more than Katie gave me.

Her mom comes out next, Aunt Feather, frowning at me or my tent as she descends rigidly down the stairs. At her heels, Uncle Glen, his hips so wide they barely fit through the narrow door, grinning at me the way he grins at everyone. I wave, turn back to my stake, and raise the rock. It crumbles over the metal, not a rock but a clod.

To the side, where he's been running in circles, Jett cackles. I see him bending to look for his own clod.

"Where's my babies?" a voice calls out, and I stand, turning, to see Meemaw.

One thing about my Meemaw is that all of us are her babies, whether literal babies or literally hers or not. Her smile isn't quite warm—I've always thought she must have so much restraint built into the deep lines of her made-up face—but her voice is. She's a slender, strong woman, with posture doing noble battle with a stoop curling her upper spine into an elegant question mark. I've never seen her in a hoodie in my life, but she looks comfortable in it paired with creased slacks and nice hiking boots. Her lips are the same unnatural shade of red as her hair, smooth and stiff around a pair of ear covers that clamp up and under her bob instead of over her head.

"Hi, Meemaw," I say, standing to hug her. She feels slight in my arms, which catches me off guard. Every time I see her, she seems older than the time before. I guess it's been a little over a year this time.

"Hi Kasper," she says, patting my arm. "How you doing, baby?"

"Good."

"Here you go." She pulls a folded hoodie from under one arm and hands it to me. I feel my eyebrows jump, and she smiles magnanimously at me. "Meemaw knows." She winks.

Before I can even thank her, she calls out, "Jett, don't get all dirty before the photos!"

I glance to see him narrowly dodge a clod that he must've tossed straight up in the air. It fragments a foot from his sneaker, and he runs away.

Meemaw hugs Dylan too, commenting as always on how tall he is, and then she says, "I'm so glad we're all here. Thanks for making the drives. Now, everyone put your phones in the cloche." She points to an oversized glass goblet on the camp table that has a large dome lid sitting beside it. There are already several phones in it, so she must be talking to me and Dylan. With a sigh, I pull it from my pocket, power it off, and place it gingerly in with the rest. My brother does the same, but Charlotte needs some prompting. She's texting until the last minute, when she finally puts it in at a throat-clearing from Meemaw.

"Jett," she calls out to my nine-year-old cousin. "You too."

He buzzes through the grown ups like an airplane. "I don't have a phone yet, Meemaw. Mom won't let me!"

Norma nods, shrugging, but Meemaw says, "That thing you were playing on earlier. In it goes."

Jett stops. "That's not a phone."

Meemaw points to the second line on the wooden sign. "What's that say?"

Jett sighs, flicks a frown at the sign and then at his grandma.

"No screens," he pouts. At his tone, Meemaw drops her red-nailed finger to the line that says, *No whining*. He scowls, but goes up the RV stairs, presumably to get whatever device Meemaw was talking about.

"Alright, Cliff?" Meemaw says to my dad. "Where do you want us?"

Dad has his nice, professional-style digital camera and a tripod out. He's already got it set up pointing at the vista beyond our campground, with the canyons rising in the background like tired mountain ranges, and above them that impossibly wide stretch of sky. He points to an open patch, where two juniper trees naturally frame the background. "I'm thinking lined up right over there. How many are we?" he asks.

"Eleven?" Mom asks, leading the way. "Greg couldn't make it." Greg is my sister's new husband, Wyatt's dad.

"Twelve if you count the baby," Norma says.

Katie says in a falsely cheerful voice, "Of course we count Wyatt." She kisses his hooded head defensively. Someone has ordered him a tiny ginger onesie.

"Twelve," Mom apologizes.

"Eleven and a half?" Dad quips, and if anyone else had said it, Katie might've glared, but she and Dad have always shared an easiness, so she smiles, only pretending to roll her eyes.

Jett barrels out of the RV, defeatedly drops a handheld gaming device into the glass dome, and races to be the first one to the photo spot. Meemaw puts the lid on the cloche, has Dad lift it into an exterior storage compartment in the bottom of the camper, and then ceremoniously locks it.

I stuff my raincoat and green sweater into my mostly-pitched tent before tugging on Meemaw's spare hoodie. I adjust my beanie and bring my hair forward over one shoulder so I don't look bald in the shot. Nearly-neon orange is not my color. I wonder which of my aunts made this particular decision, but it was probably in the emails I should've read, so I won't ask.

Leaning over his camera to peer through the viewing window, Dad calls out instructions to line up the long row of my family so they'll all fit in the shot. He puts Dylan near the middle because of his height, arranging nuclear family groups logically out from that, with only baby Wyatt doubling the row. As I walk up behind him, I see what he's doing. The sun is behind them all, but he's got a cool, artsy, backlit situation going where the row of us will be almost silhouetted against the striking scenery behind us.

"Don't forget to leave a spot for me," he calls.

"And me," I echo, and he jumps.

He looks over his shoulder, clearly having forgotten I wasn't in the line yet. "Right, and Kassie. Maybe on the end there, beside Katie and Wyatt."

I nod, tucking my head down against a sudden gust of wind that howls through the canyon as I trudge toward my assigned side. It's probably just how many of us there are, and nothing personal. That's what I tell myself as I move to stand on the far end of the line.

Dad is far enough away that I can't make out his muttering as he sets up whatever camera specifics he cares about. Exposure, a timer, whatever. Then he raises his voice: "Everyone hold hands?"

I sense the shuffling of us all. Katie is to my left, but her right arm is taken by holding Wyatt. I look at him. He stares at me with big, soft blue eyes. I swipe a drip of drool from his mouth with my sleeve cuff, and he slowly blinks before looking up at his mom as if to check if I'm dangerous.

Unaware or unconcerned that I don't have a hand to hold, Dad calls, "Glen, step to the left—sorry, your right—so I can see you and Charlotte's hands in the gap. Yeah, good. And Mom? You and Colleen scooch a tad closer together. Right. Then I'll hop in between Colleen and Dylan. Perfect. Okay, I'll run into place. We have ten seconds, then it will take several shots in a row. Everyone smile!"

I watch as Dad scurries toward the middle of the line to shuffle into place, laughing, "Don't everyone lean to look! Look at the camera!"

This will be a gift from Meemaw, I'm sure. She'll frame them and either drop off or mail us each one, depending on how long our drives are. My money's on receiving them by actual Christmas.

I should speak up, I guess. I told myself I would. I could get Katie to switch sides with me so that the baby is at the end, her arm holding him to conclude the line instead of both of my hands hanging emptily by my sides. But as I force a facsimile of a smile into my cheeks, I can't make myself. It's not worth the drama, their annoyance at having to take another shot. Maybe it's my speaking up about these little things that makes them feel like I'm always inconveniencing, disrupting.

And who cares, really? I have the defeating certainty that if I weren't here, no one would even notice the difference. I'll save speaking up for something bigger, more important.

The camera clicks several times in a row, rapid-fire.

THANKS FOR READING!

For more great Shortwave titles, visit us online. . .

OUR WEBSITE
shortwavepublishing.com

SOCIAL MEDIA
@shortwavebooks

EMAIL US
contact@shortwavepublishing.com